*"I have everyth___
except someo___*

The yearning in Morgan's eyes made her turn away. Denise felt a bit sorry that she had asked, a little panicked, even, because something seemed to flutter in her chest when he looked at her like that, something she was too mature to feel.

She had to remind herself this was business. They were only pretending to date. So what if in an unguarded moment he made her heart beat a little faster? So what if the night was dark and soft, and she felt cocooned in luxury and utterly feminine for the first time in so long, and the smile on Morgan's face and the appreciation in his eyes caused a secret little thrill deep within her? So what?

So she was in trouble. That was what.

Dear Reader,

Happy Valentine's Day! What better way to celebrate than with a Silhouette Romance novel? We're sweeter than chocolate—and less damaging to the hips! This month is filled with special treats just for you. LOVING THE BOSS, our six-book series about office romances that lead to happily ever after, continues with *The Night Before Baby* by Karen Rose Smith. In this sparkling story, an unforgettable one-night stand—during the company Christmas party!—leads to an unexpected pregnancy and a must-read marriage of convenience.

Teresa Southwick crafts an emotional BUNDLES OF JOY title, in which the forbidden man of her dreams becomes a pregnant woman's stand-in groom. Don't miss *A Vow, a Ring, a Baby Swing.* When a devil-may-care bachelor discovers he's a daddy, he offers the prim heroine a chance to hold a *Baby in Her Arms,* as Judy Christenberry's LUCKY CHARM SISTERS trilogy resumes.

Award-winning author Marie Ferrarella proves it's *Never Too Late for Love* as the bride's mother and the groom's widower father discover their children's wedding was just the beginning in this charming continuation of LIKE MOTHER, LIKE DAUGHTER. Beloved author Arlene James lends a traditional touch to Silhouette Romance's ongoing HE'S MY HERO promotion with *Mr. Right Next Door.* And FAMILY MATTERS spotlights new talent Elyssa Henry with her heartwarming debut, *A Family for the Sheriff.*

Treat yourself to each and every offering this month. And in future months, look for more of the stories you love…and the authors you cherish.

Enjoy!

Mary-Theresa Hussey

Mary-Theresa Hussey
Senior Editor, Silhouette Romance

Please address questions and book requests to:
Silhouette Reader Service
U.S.: 3010 Walden Ave., P.O. Box 1325, Buffalo, NY 14269
Canadian: P.O. Box 609, Fort Erie, Ont. L2A 5X3

Arlene James

MR. RIGHT NEXT DOOR

Silhouette
ROMANCE™
Published by Silhouette Books
America's Publisher of Contemporary Romance

SILHOUETTE BOOKS

ISBN 0-373-19352-1

MR. RIGHT NEXT DOOR

Printed in U.S.A.

Books by Arlene James

ARLENE JAMES

grew up in Oklahoma and has lived all over the South. In 1976 she married "the most romantic man in the world." The author enjoys traveling with her husband, but writing has always been her chief pastime.

MISSOURI

OKLAHOMA

Jasper

Fayetteville

Fort Smith

Little Rock ★

ARKANSAS

All underlined places are fictitious.

TEXAS

LOUISIANA

MISSISSIPPI

TENNESSEE

Chapter One

The ball ricocheted off the wall with a satisfying thwack, hurtling to her left. It would take a twisting eight-foot lunge to return it, but she had no doubt that she could manage. It was a move she'd made before. She had already begun the motion when she remembered that the politic action would be to let that ball pass. Her arm was already extended, the racquet at the perfect angle, with only a split second to act. Too late to abort the movement. Too late to correct—or rather, corrupt—the angle. In desperation, she did the only thing she could. She simply let go. The racquet hit the floor at the same instant she did, bounced off the rubber grip on the handle, and clattered to a rest, while Denise herself slid across the floor to collide with the wall, sprawling in an inelegant heap of bare limbs, coffee brown ponytail and athletic shoes. Chuck's triumphant laughter echoed around the court. Denise felt a flare of resentment quickly followed by the stinging of friction-burned skin and the cool, studied control that kept her sane.

Gingerly, she righted herself and sat up, back braced against the wall, chest heaving. Well, she told herself, she could take satisfaction in the fact that he'd never know that she'd let him win. She'd had him worried this time, too, made him suffer. That counted for something. She flexed one knee, balanced a forearm atop it and concentrated on getting air into her beleaguered body. Chuck, meanwhile, stood bent over with his hands on his thighs, gasping and huffing, his slightly jowly face almost purple, sweat rolling off of the top of his balding head to drip on the floor. Denise was back to normal and checking over her racquet for damage long before Chuck regained enough strength and breath to rub in her loss.

"And old Dennis bites the dust again!" he said, finally. It was the office joke, calling her Dennis. Chuck shook his racquet at her and added patronizingly, "But you're definitely getting better, though. Definite improvement."

Denise smiled mechanically. Little did the old goat know that she could take him anytime she wanted. Did being the boss blind you to such lowering conclusions? she wondered. She made a mental note never to fall victim to such ego-enhancing vision herself. When her turn came—and it would, she was determined about that—she'd be a far superior manager than Chuck Dayton and his cronies, but then a woman had to be better just to be considered par. She sighed and for a moment allowed herself to be weary of the whole ugly, convoluted struggle that was her life. Then she put away the self-pity, squared her shoulders, wiped the perspiration from her brow and reminded herself that she was a woman with goals, and that at thirty-five she could handily whip her overbearing boss's fifty-year-old butt at racquetball any day of the week. Heck, she worked harder at letting him win than winning herself, and one day he'd know it.

Retrieving her towel and wiping her face, she listened with half an ear as Chuck berated her—under the guise of helpful camaraderie—for her "lack of control" for dropping her racquet. She made noises of protest and regret, but apparently she wasn't humiliated enough to properly feed Chuck's need for superiority, for he somehow evaded her finely honed senses of warning and moved close enough to get a hand on her bottom and whisper in her ear, "Bet you never drop the ball between the sheets, though."

Before she could sling an elbow at him, he moved away, chuckling and no doubt congratulating himself on his cleverness. Denise contented herself with muttered threats and a stern reminder that she could take anything that Chuck Dayton could dish out—and one day, somehow, someway, she'd make him pay for every sexist, sleazy remark. Two months she'd worked for him, from the very day she'd gotten to town, and the list was growing longer every day. She'd been warned, of course. Chuck liked to chew up his subordinates and spit them out. Those who buckled were sent down to dead-end jobs on the backside of nowhere. Those who didn't often found themselves on the fast track to corporate heaven. Denise meant not only to breach the pearly gates of said heaven but to take a blatantly superior cloud for her own. Within five years—by the age of forty—she intended to be the top female officer in the company. With that happy thought lightening her mood, she slipped out the door to the prep room and dropped onto a bench, where she zipped her racquet into its leather case and took off her shoes before padding lightly on stockinged feet toward the women's lockers.

A man pushed away from the wall and stepped smack into her path. Denise literally recoiled, some sixth sense recognizing her handsome landlord even before her gaze focused in on his face. Every alarm bell in her system was clanging a warning, as it had from the moment she'd met this irritatingly persistent, if somewhat charming, man.

"Good game," he said heartily. "Must be hard to lose when you're so obviously the better player."

Satisfaction stabbed through her, but she repressed it

ruthlessly by taking the opposite tack, a technique that often worked for her. "Don't be absurd. Chuck's the big dog around here. But I almost got him this time. Next time for sure."

"Yeah, right. Want some real competition? I promise not to let you win."

Morgan Holt smirked and folded his well-tanned arms, the hair on them glowing pale yellow, despite the chestnut brown waves that flowed back from a slightly peaked hairline, the temples streaked lightly with gray. She had noticed before, and couldn't help thinking again, how those tiny streaks of gray brought out the pale blue of his eyes. There went those clanging bells again. She stepped to the side, ducking her head and saying, "I have to get home."

"To whom?" he said cryptically. "Your cat?"

Anger surged through her. Blast him, why didn't he take her hints and back off? Did he get some kind of charge out of dancing too close to the flame? Well, she could burn him if that's what it would take. She mimicked his stance and his expression, folding her arms and flexing one knee, her smirk particularly acidic. "My cat's far better company than anyone I know," she said pointedly.

The wretch laughed. "But can it play a mean game of racquetball?"

Suddenly Denise was aching to slam that ball around the room or, preferably, right into his face. He was nothing and nobody to her. She wouldn't have to hold back. She could give free rein to her competitiveness and just go for it. He was unlike Chuck Dayton in another way, though. Physically Chuck was maybe average in athletic conditioning and ability. Morgan was probably a decade younger in age and in far superior shape. Athletic ability seemed a given. Still, she had at least a few years on him, and, though at five foot five she was only of average height, she had a great deal more muscle mass, percentagewise, than most people. Plus, her reflexes were quick and sharp.

She might not be able to beat him, but she could do to him what she'd done to Chuck. She could make him work for it far harder than he expected to.

"I just had a strenuous game," she pointed out, hoping to create a little overconfidence in him.

He shrugged. "I just cut down that old tree behind your patio that you were so worried about, plus I corded and stacked the wood."

Denise lifted a brow. She had to give him credit for being a good landlord. He maintained and serviced the small apartment building in which she lived with the same promptness and loving care that he lavished on his restored Victorian home, which was part of the same property. She had had reservations about living right behind her landlord, but Jasper, Arkansas, was a small town, and unless she wanted to make the daily thirty-plus-mile drive from and to Fayetteville, choices were limited. She'd figured that living within a few hundred yards of the office outweighed any negatives of having her landlord so close. As far as the apartment went, having Morgan Holt on the premises had proven far more convenient than she had anticipated. Personally, however, the arrangement was anything but comfortable. He'd made it plain almost from the beginning that he found her attractive, and she'd tried to make it equally as obvious that she wasn't interested. So why was she standing here intending to accept his challenge? Because, she told herself, the opportunity for a little honest competition came all too rarely into her life. And because she had a good chance of waxing his butt, which just might have a dampening effect on his interest. She'd be nuts not to play him. Heavens, she might never again have such an opportunity!

"You're on."

He grinned, blue eyes sparkling. "Court three. Ten minutes." Still grinning cheekily, he strolled away, worn court shoes dangling over one shoulder by the strings. He was showing an indecent amount of tanned skin with his faded black shorts and ragged gray sweatshirt with the sleeves cut out and the sides slashed all the way to the band at the bottom. She shook her head, wondering if any other man of her acquaintance could look so good in such unfashionable garb. Most of the members here liked to keep up with the latest trends and styles, believing science ultimately drove the market in sports gear. A new thought struck. Members. Morgan Holt couldn't be a member here. This was a company club reserved for employees and their immediate family members. She supposed that he could have a relative at Wholesale International, but he'd been specific about being single, so it couldn't be a spouse. More likely he was someone's guest, but whose?

Curious, she left her shoes on the end of a bench and walked briskly out to the sign-in desk. Someone had to have reserved court three. Glancing at the clock above it, she took the clipboard off the wall and flipped up the top sheet, trailing her gaze down the time column until she came to 6:15 p.m., then following it across to the proper court column. There, written in pencil, was her own name. She dropped her jaw. The goat had reserved the court in her name! How presumptuous! How audacious! How infuriatingly nervy! How opportunistic. She slammed the clipboard in its place and turned back the way she'd come, eyes narrowed with determination. Oh, man, she wasn't just going to wax him, she was going to kill him, annihilate him, embarrass him. When she was through with him, he wouldn't want to so much as show his cheeky face around here, let alone sneak in claiming her sponsorship! Oh, and she was going to enjoy it. She was going to enjoy it very much.

He knew three minutes after she entered the room that she was unbeatable. He recognized the determination, the utter ruthlessness beneath the fluidity of her stride and the implacable glitter of her exotically tilted, dark brown eyes. She'd come for his hide, and he rather expected that she'd get it. The thought made him grin, not that he would make it easy for her. Oh, no. Instinct told him that Denise Jenkins survived on challenge. She needed it on some emotional level that he hadn't plumbed yet. Then again, she hadn't given him much of a chance, nor was she likely to unless he could wiggle his way beneath that prickly exterior. A smitten man wasn't much challenge, as it happened, so he had to find other ways to engage her interest. He had the feeling he'd outdone himself this time. He could imagine the sore muscles that would greet him on the morrow. He bounced the ball against the floor and prepared himself for a grueling workout.

She didn't disappoint. Not only was the pace manic, the game was almost brutally physical. She meant to win at any cost, and the collisions and jabs and tripping feet were just part of it. She drove him to the wall more times than he could count, and her racquet whiffed his ear close enough to burn. He left a yard of skin on the floor and ripped what was left of his shirt into pieces, so that he wound up tossing it into a pile in a corner and playing bare from the waist up. When the end came, it found him face-down on the floor spread-eagled in a vain attempt to save the point, while she jogged backward and prepared herself to bury the ball in the wall—or his back. He sighed with relief when she let it go, dropping her racquet and relaxing her stance. Recognizing the sounds of her approach, he forced himself to roll over, groaning with the effort. Just then breathing was about all he could manage. He tried to sit up, but lifting his head a few inches was about the limit of his body's cooperation.

Denise Jenkins loomed over him from a height of maybe five and a half feet. Her hair had pulled free of her ponytail in dark, silky locks and hung limply around a face red with exertion, while her sleeveless tank top was plastered to her firm body with the same sweat that slid down her slender neck in droplets. Her fingers were locked around the handle of her racquet, the knuckles white as she gasped for air through an open mouth. He envied her the energy required to sink down onto her haunches and give him a smug smile. She was gorgeous.

"Don't you…just hate…to be bested…by a woman?" she asked between puffs of breath.

He left his racquet on his chest and managed to stack his hands beneath his head. "Naw," he said panting for air. "Not me." He took another puff. "I love a woman who—" and another puff "—can hold her own."

"Hold her own?" She finally released her grip on her racquet and used it for support as she pushed up to her full height. "I beat you…in case you weren't counting."

"I was counting," he said, managing to push himself up onto his arms, the heels of his hands braced against the floor. "Next time I'll be sure I'm fresh."

"No next time," she said flatly. "You had your shot. One's all you get."

Morgan came up to balance one forearm on a knee. "Afraid I'll take you if we play again?"

She shook her head, catching the rubber band as her thick, shoulder-length hair slid free. "You aren't listening. We won't play again. And if I find out that you've used my name to get into the gym again, I'll report you."

He chuckled. "You do that. But it kind of begs the question, doesn't it?"

"What question?"

"Was it skill and stamina or pure luck?"

She pointed a stern finger at him. "I beat you fair and square."

"Agreed. But can you do it again?"

She went down on her haunches once more, her weight balanced easily on the balls of her feet this time. "You just don't get it, do you? We're not chums, you and I, bashing a ball around the court in a friendly game. We're landlord and tenant and nothing more.''

"That's easily corrected,'' he said smoothly. "How about dinner?''

Her face went perfectly rigid before she pushed up to stand over him again. "No, thanks.''

"Aw, come on, Denise. What's a guy got to do to get on with you?''

She gave him a bored look and turned away, saying, "I'm not in a dating mode, if you must know. My job takes up most of my time.''

"I used to be like that,'' he said cryptically, leaning back and crossing one ankle over the other. That piqued her interest enough to make her glance over one shoulder.

"Oh, really? What happened? You miss the big promotion?''

He just grinned at that. "Why don't you come to dinner and find out?''

She rolled her eyes and moved toward the door. "I have enough to do just keeping up with my own career, thank you. Oh, and by the way—'' she turned back to smile at him "—your dog has a habit of leaving large, smelly gifts on my front walk. See to it that he stops, will you?'' With that she opened the door and strode through it, leaving him weak and disappointed. Worse yet, he was discouraged. He was fresh out of ideas how to get next to Denise Jenkins— ideas and, it seemed, opportunity.

Denise closed the door to Chuck's office and took a deep breath, carefully keeping her facial expression stern. It wouldn't do to show the staff that old Chuck had managed to get to her. Again. Man, she'd like to push a fist into that smug, jowly face.

Looking hot today, honey. The coolest ones in the boardroom are the hottest in the bedroom. Soften the blow and flash him a little something when you do it.

She closed her eyes momentarily, dreading what she had to do. Trust Chuck to make her his hatchet man and to insult her in the process. For five cents she'd file a sexual harassment suit against him. But then she could kiss good-bye any chance of advancement, and she'd worked too hard to lose out now. Squaring her shoulders, she strode smoothly through the secretarial pool and into one of several nondescript corridors that opened into cubicle after cubicle, each as cell-like and cramped as the last. When she reached the one she sought, she rapped lightly on the empty door frame and waited for the young man inside to look up and smile at her.

"Ms. Jenkins!"

"Ken, I need a word with you please."

"Sure. What's up?"

Denise would not allow herself to smile, though the impulse to soften the blow, even to derail it, was strong. "Not here. Meet me in my office. Five minutes all right?"

She watched the implications sink in and tried not to think that Ken Walters was a young married man with a baby. According to Chuck, that was the problem. Ken wasn't giving it his all. He'd let family concerns get in the way of business. Never mind that the baby had been born prematurely with a heart ailment and this after Ken and his wife had already lost one stillborn child. It was true that Ken hadn't exactly set sales records, but surely that was understandable given the circumstances. Sales were all that counted in this business, but had it been her call to make, she'd have transferred Ken to a less stressful job until he felt able to give it his all again. Unfortunately, it wasn't her call—just her task. She strode back to her office, viciously determined to do what she could for Walters.

He barely gave her time to get off the phone. She was just hanging up the receiver when he opened the door and walked in, not bothering to have himself announced by her secretary and, thereby, letting her know that he was well aware what was coming. She didn't beat around the bush. He obviously didn't want that.

"I'm sorry, Ken. I know it's unfair, but I have to let you go."

He paled and ducked his head, balled hands going into his trouser pockets. "Damn it!"

She hit the button on the intercom. "Betty, bring in that letter the moment it's ready." She turned back to Ken Walters. "Sit down. I'm having my secretary prepare a letter of recommendation, and I've taken the liberty of making an appointment for you with a business acquaintance in Rogers." She smiled lamely. "Didn't think you'd mind." She pushed at him a piece of paper on which she'd written the details, trying to ignore the look of amazement on his face as he gingerly lowered himself into the indicated chair and pulled the paper toward him. It seemed to take forever for him to read the few words written there.

Denise cleared her throat and went on briskly. "I know insurance will be a problem because of your baby's pre-existing health problems, but I've taken that into account. I happen to know that both companies use the same insurer, and I'll do what I can—quietly—to see that you're fully covered." For the first time, she let herself smile. "Just don't blow the interview. I've opened the door but getting inside is still up to you. Understood?"

Ken Walters carefully folded the paper and slipped it into his coat pocket before looking up, eyes beaming gratitude. "It's a shame," he said quietly, "that no one around here knows what a nice person you are. You must have to work very hard at keeping it hidden."

She gulped, surprised by the lump that rose in her throat, and said, "I'd appreciate it if you wouldn't mention this to anyone."

Nodding, he got to his feet. "Don't worry. I won't blow your cover."

She smiled indulgently at that, fingers templed against

her lips. "If you hurry, you'll just have time to clear out your office and make it to the interview."

He nodded. "I don't know how to thank you. God knows I'd rather go home to my wife with the news that I've changed jobs unexpectedly instead of, 'I've been canned!'"

Denise held up a cautioning hand. "It's not a done deal. You could blow this if you go in there with the wrong attitude."

He chuckled. "Not a chance. I'm a salesman, and my top product's me. It's been a rough few months, but I'm ready to be on top of the heap again. In fact, I haven't been this raring to go since I got out of college. Maybe this chance is just what I need." He patted his pocket before saying, "I'll just pick up that letter on my way out."

Denise got up and extended her hand. Ken took it in both of his, held it, and said meaningfully. "Thank you. I won't forget this." And then he walked out of her office, his step decidedly more spry than when he'd come in. As the door closed behind him, Denise felt an overwhelming sense of loss.

It didn't make much sense. Ken Walters had never been a buddy. She was his superior. He had only this moment begun to think of her as even human, and that had been completely by her own design, so then why should she feel lonely now that he was gone? Nothing had really changed. Nothing would. She had her career, and that was all she needed. Wasn't it?

Denise watched out her window as Morgan whizzed the Frisbee through the air, laughing as his big dog Reiver launched his ninety-pound body into flight and snatched it in his powerful jaws, white teeth flashing against his brown-and-black muzzle. The dog landed lightly on all fours and loped toward him, ears flopping. Morgan opened his arms and bent forward in offer of reward. Reiver leaped at him, knocking him flat on his back and depositing the disk on his chest before lapping his face with a long, pink tongue. Morgan howled, trying to fend off the dog and hug him at the same time, too weak with laughter to do anything but endure. Then he turned his head and saw her, and the laughter died. Denise felt a twinge of guilt for having ruined his mood. He pushed the dog off and sat up, staring at her window. She tried not to let on that she had been watching, sipping from a coffee cup and petting her cat with one hand. Obviously he couldn't stand the sight of her now. He got up and went into the house.

Denise turned away from the window with a sigh. She should be glad. She hadn't wanted his attentions or any man's, so what was wrong with her? It wasn't like her to feel so…bereft. Well, not in a long time, not since she'd so painstakingly rebuilt her life, not since… She got up from the armchair, unceremoniously dumping the cat from her lap, and wandered over to the bookshelf, torn between taking down the photograph album and passing it by. She took it down, set aside her cup and opened the cover.

Jeremy smiled up at her, a little blob of baby fat in a blue one-piece shorty, that little eyebrow quirked just so. She turned the page. Jeremy pushed his walker around the room clad only in his diaper, his little face utterly gleeful. She couldn't bear any more. She closed the book and briefly hugged it to her before sliding it back into place on the shelf. She couldn't bear to see again how he'd grown and changed and matured, how the baby fat had gradually become thin, hard little muscles, how his face beamed with secret knowledge and avid intelligence. She couldn't bear, especially, that the pictures would stop there, frozen in time forever. At eight. There would never be a picture of Jeremy at ten or twelve or twenty-one. There would never be another picture of Jeremy ever. She closed her eyes against the searing pain, no longer expecting it to soften or lessen. The years had shown her that losing one's child never got easier or better.

A knock at her door provided welcome distraction. She left her cup where it was, wrapped her sweater tightly about her and walked into the tiny foyer to answer it. Morgan Holt smiled down at her, a casserole balanced on one palm.

"Got a minute?"

A minute? she thought wryly, pathetically grateful that she had misjudged him. Old habits died hard, however, and she heard herself saying, "Just. I have some paperwork to go over tonight and—" The cat made a bid for the door, slinking between her ankles and elongating its stride. "Smithson, get back here!" She caught at the regal blue-gray tail. Morgan quickly stepped inside and pulled the door closed.

The cat immediately twined itself around his ankles, meowing. "Russian blue?" Morgan asked, maneuvering the casserole in order to look down at the cat.

"Somewhere along the way, I imagine," Denise said, leaning down and plucking up the cat. He was a big, arrogant male, completely unconcerned that he'd been declawed and fixed. At a sleek fourteen pounds, he considered himself emperor of the world even though he seldom left the apartment and only then in a locked carrier. He ducked his head and turned away as Denise attempted to stroke between his ears. To further indicate his disdain, he hooked his only remaining claws, those of his back paws, into her abdomen and pushed away, leaping to the floor and wrapping his long body around Morgan's ankles in another examination of the door.

Morgan laughed. "What'd you say his name was?"

"Smithson."

"Smithson?"

"Yeah, as in 'son of Smith.'"

"Ah, so his father's name was Smith."

Denise lifted both brows in a gesture of surprise. "Very good. Most people don't get it."

"That you had a cat named Smith," Morgan clarified, "and now have raised one of his kittens."

"Exactly."

He smiled. "There, see, we have more in common than racquetball and residence."

"And that would be?"

"Obviously we're both animal lovers."

Denise made a doubtful face. "I imagine we're about as compatible as cats and dogs."

He laughed. "You never know."

But she did. She felt certain that she did, and instinctively she began turning away.

"Uh, about this," he said, holding aloft the steaming ceramic dish. "It's an apology. I shouldn't have used your name to get into the gym without your permission. I'm sorry. Sort of."

She couldn't help smiling. Sorry, sort of? What kind of apology was that? She said, "Funny, it doesn't seem much like an apology. Actually, it looks and smells like a casserole."

He laughed. "An apology casserole. I thought...I hoped... Well, let's just say I'm reconciled to being friends. Casual friends."

Denise was unprepared for the disappointment that arrowed through her, but she instantly dismissed it, seizing instead on the peace offering. Friends, even casual friends, was something of a compromise, but she wouldn't let herself think of that, not tonight. She peered down into the casserole dish. "What is it?"

"Chicken," he said, "all white meat, cheese, rice, broccoli and cauliflower. Very low fat."

It smelled wonderful, but she lifted an eyebrow at the low-fat part. "Low-fat cheese?"

He sketched a cross over his heart. "And skim milk. Scout's honor."

She eyed him warily. He didn't look much like he needed to worry about things like fat in his diet. She remembered the hard, well-defined muscles of his bare chest and thighs, and for some reason the memory made her uncomfortable. She motioned for him to follow her into the kitchen, saying, "Am I suppose to believe that you eat so sensibly all the time?"

He slid the casserole and the hot pad on which he carried it onto the countertop, slapping his flat middle. "Hey, keeping in shape at forty-five isn't as easy as you might think. You'll find out one of these days."

Forty-five. She blurted, "You're older than I thought."

He grinned. "Thanks."

She quickly washed her hands before pulling a plate out of the cupboard, then she reached up and pulled out another. What the heck. Even casual friendship required some reciprocation. She took out glasses, flatware, and napkins and set the table in silence. When she looked up, he said, "Am I being invited to dinner?"

"Friends do that, don't they? On occasion."

He chuckled. "On occasion. But what about the paperwork?"

She halted, ashamed suddenly of the lie, and stammered, "Uh, i-it c-can wait."

He shrugged and clapped his hands together, rubbing them briskly. "Okay, so, got any bread? A little salad maybe?"

She pointed to a cabinet door, then opened the refrigerator and looked inside. "I've got some greens, but there doesn't seem to be any dressing."

He took a bottle of red wine from the cabinet along with the bread, hefted it in one hand lightly and said, "I think I can take care of that. May I?" He indicated her pantry with a jerk of his head.

She took out the salad and set it on the counter, saying, "Knock yourself out."

He went to work, and it became quickly obvious that he knew very well what he was doing and enjoyed it. To her, cooking was a chore that she often chose not to perform. Morgan not only enjoyed it but reveled in it, and the results reflected that. Sitting at the table with seasoned toast, salad dressed with red wine and spices, and a cheesy chicken casserole, Denise found herself smiling for the first time in days. Her smile turned into a hum of pleasure as she forked casserole into her mouth.

Morgan smiled knowingly and said, "Good isn't it? Want the recipe?"

She shook her head then said, "Yes, it's good. No, I don't want the recipe."

"Don't like to cook, huh?"

She shrugged. "Don't have the time."

He ate thoughtfully for a few seconds, then laid aside his fork and said, "I know what you mean. I always enjoyed cooking, but then I got so caught up in that whole corporate career thing that cooking—and just about everything else I enjoyed—fell by the wayside."

"Well, but if you enjoyed your career—"

"I didn't. Oh, it had its moments. I got addicted in a way to the thrill of the deal, you know, the one-upmanship, the winning. Then one day it occurred to me that if I, quote, won, unquote, someone else had to lose, and in so many cases it just wasn't necessary. I started wondering why it couldn't be a win-win situation at least some of the time, and I was told in no uncertain terms that I had lost my edge, that business always was and always would be about, and again I quote, going in for the kill."

He went back to eating, but she couldn't help feeling that he'd left the story unfinished. "So what happened?" she prodded, irritated when he took his time chewing and swallowing.

"What happened was, my wife insisted I go in for counseling. She couldn't understand why I was unhappy, and she was convinced that the problem was all in my head."

"And?"

"And the counselor possessed a very open mind. It only took a few sessions for both of us to understand that I'd been trying for years to fit a mold fashioned for me by someone else."

Denise couldn't help a spurt of resentment. She flattened her lips. "So it was all the wife's fault, I suppose?"

He shook his head. "No, it was all my fault. I should have stood on my own values and principles from the beginning, but I wanted to make her happy. I didn't see that mutual love, real love, accepts. Eventually we both realized that we didn't really love each other. I was dazzled by her sophistication in the beginning, and what attracted her to me was my willingness to let her mold me into what she thought she ought to have in a husband. When I was no longer dazzled and no longer willing…"

Denise finished for him, "The marriage fell apart."

He nodded, leaned both elbows on the table and linked his hands over his plate. "What about you?"

Denise immediately felt the old wariness rise. "Me?"

"Umm-hmm, you ever been married?"

She briefly considered several replies, from an outright lie to flatly telling him it was none of his business, but then, she'd just elicited his story from him, so that hardly seemed fair. She kept her eyes on her plate and her fork busy as she said, "I was married."

"Divorced?" he asked quietly.

"Yes."

"I guess you don't want to tell me why," he said after a moment, and she knew that the disappointment in his tone had less to do with curiosity than the fact that their so-called friendship was not turning out to be exactly reciprocal.

She took a deep breath. "I got pregnant."

It took several moments for that to sink in. Once it did, he dropped his hands to his lap and said, "I thought getting pregnant was a reason to get married, not divorced."

The old bitterness filled her and she vented it with sarcasm. "That's usually how it works, yeah, but not with my ex."

"I'm afraid I don't understand that," Morgan said softly.

She gave up the pretense of eating and sat back in her chair, lifting her gaze to his. "We got married right out of college, top of our class, roaring to go. We were going to set the business world on its ear. No mention was ever made of children. I suppose I thought we'd conquer the business world and then move on to parenthood. Then I got a terrible sinus infection, and the doctor failed to tell me that the antibiotic I was on could affect the birth control pills I was taking. At first I just couldn't believe I'd gotten pregnant. Then when the shock wore off I couldn't help thinking like a mother, you know?"

"I know. I have a son of my own."

She managed to smile at that. "I'm glad. I wish… Well, not anymore, but at the time I thought that if only Derek would be glad, everything would be wonderful."

"But Derek wasn't glad," Morgan stated gently.

She marshaled the words in her head, still not quite able to reconcile them. "Derek gave me the option of abortion or divorce."

"And you chose divorce."

"I chose to have my baby, even if it meant having him alone."

"Him? You have a son, too?"

She forced her tongue to form the single word. "Had."

A heartbeat later, Morgan Holt did what no one else had

ever done. He got up from his seat and walked around the table, where he knelt beside her, took her hands in his and gently said, ''I'm so sorry. Would you like to tell me about him?''

Chapter Two

Denise took up the pen and began writing her name on the appropriate line, and right in the middle of *Jenkins,* she completely forgot what she was doing. Her mind flashed on that moment when he had knelt by her chair and taken her hands in his. Her memory played for her a vision of blue, blue eyes so misty with understanding, so warm, that looking into them had seemed to melt something hard and icy deep within her. She couldn't quite believe that, with tears rolling down her face, she had begun telling Morgan about the hit-and-run, even how she had resented that the other boys, three in all, had managed to escape with various degrees of injury, while her own son had died instantly. She had never told another soul that, and over the years she had felt genuine shame for her private reaction to the survival of those other boys. Now she was left wondering if anyone other than Morgan Holt would have accepted that confession with the same equanimity and nonjudgmental compassion as he had shown her that night, and the idea that he might be unique in even that one way somehow terrified her so badly that her hands shook.

"Ms. Jenkins?"

Her secretary's concerned voice jerked her back to the present. Denise started and dropped the pen.

"Are you all right?"

Embarrassment started a burning sensation at the base of her throat, but Denise ignored the color threatening to climb to her face and picked up the pen again, murmuring, "Just a cramp in my hand." She quickly finished her signature and pushed away the papers. "Anything else, Betty?"

"Just your meeting with Mr. Dayton."

Denise glanced at her wristwatch and got up from her desk, briskly but not quite successfully suppressing her dread. "I expect the meeting will flow over into lunch," she said absently, "so you might as well go ahead and take your break now. I know you must want to check on your granddaughter."

Betty had been gathering up the papers strewn over the top of Denise's desk. It was the sudden cessation of her quick, efficient movements that alerted Denise. She looked up, catching Betty's expression of surprise just before the older woman masked it. Irritation made Denise snap, "Well, she is having her tonsils out, isn't she?"

"Yes, ma'am. I just… That is, thank you. Thank you very much."

Denise waved her away with a frown, uncertain what irritated her most, that her secretary had thought she ignored the talk going around the office or her surprise at what was ultimately a meaningless bit of compassion. It cost Denise nothing, after all, if her secretary left the office a few minutes early when the woman was both efficient to the point of amazement and, at present, unneeded. Yet, Denise was embarrassingly aware herself that it was unlike her to make unnecessary comments. Normally she would have stopped with merely telling Betty to take an early lunch, making no comment about her young granddaughter's minor surgery. She couldn't think what had changed inside her that would allow, even compel, her to comment about something as private as her secretary's granddaughter. Knowing that Betty's thoughts must be somewhere along the same line as hers, she swept out of the office without so much as a glance over her shoulder.

By the time she reached Chuck's impressively swank office suite her dread had coalesced into potent distaste, and again she had no adequate explanation for her own reactions. She had never liked Chuck, but personal preference had never played a part in her career. She had always been able to keep personality out of professional dealings. What difference did it make if the boss or even a subordinate was a jerk and a bore? Or even if he was a prince and a sweetheart? All that mattered professionally, the bottom line, was performance. Period. So why suddenly should her skin crawl at the idea of walking into a room with Chuck Dayton?

She knew that Chuck was about due for a hit on her. She'd recognized the signs that announced he was working up to it. His wouldn't be the first pass she'd had to field, nor would it be the last. Denise considered such unpleasantness merely part of the job. It came with the territory, so to speak, with being a woman in a man's world. It was just one more thing that she would not let get in her way. Reminding herself of that seemed to help, so mentally she squared her shoulders, nodded at Chuck's young, nubile secretary, and marched into the lion's den.

The "lion" looked up and boomed a hearty welcome. "Hey, Dennis, come on in!"

She reminded herself that he called her Dennis because she dared to compete with the men on their own level, and it wasn't just the racquetball.

Resisting the urge to lift a hand to smooth the sleek roll of dark hair twisted against the back of her head, she instead kept her hands free and her movements fluid as she approached the desk. No chair had ever been drawn up in front of that desk. In Chuck's mind, no subordinate rated a chair at his desk, while superiors rated five-star treatment in the comfortable seating area arranged artfully before the picture window with its lovely view of the Ozarks. Chuck and only Chuck sat at that desk. Denise came to a halt in front of it and folded her arms.

"You wanted to see me?"

He shot her a knowing smirk and turned his attention back to the papers in front of him, just showing her who was boss. When he'd felt that he'd kept her waiting long enough, he looked up and smiled.

"Looking good today."

She let the compliment pass without comment. He leaned back in his chair, clearly enjoying his comfort at her expense.

"You know, you really have to loosen up. That ice queen stuff's good for the grunts. Keeps them in their place. But the higher-ups are used to living in the sun. We like a little warmth every now and again, even some real heat once in a while. I'm sure you catch my drift."

She ignored his "drift" and went straight to business. "What was it you wanted to see me about?"

Chuck frowned, then sat forward again and briskly began giving her the details. "It's about the new retailer coming on-line. I've invited the rep to dinner on Friday night at the Ozark Springs Inn. Have you been there yet?"

"Ozark Springs Inn? No, I haven't."

"Well, here's your chance to enjoy the amenities at company's expense. I think we can swing an overnight stay—for both of us."

Denise's stomach turned sour. "Your wife ought to enjoy that," she said as offhandedly as she could manage.

"My wife is used to my, uh, work keeping me out overnight." Chuck smiled and waggled his eyebrows.

It was all Denise could do to keep from gagging. Instead,

she made herself smile and pass a limp hand over her forehead. "Gee, I wish you'd given me a bit more notice,"
she said, thinking furiously. "Friday is…day after tomorrow, and I've, ah, already made plans."

The smile turned upside down. "What kind of plans?"

"Well, p-personal plans."

He screwed up his face. "A date? You're telling me you
have a *boyfriend?*"

He made it sound like a disease, and suddenly she knew
why. A boyfriend would mess up all the plans he'd been
neatly laying, plans designed to get her off by herself, plans
to seduce her. No, Chuck wouldn't go to all the trouble of
being sure that she was willing. More likely, what he had
in mind was something along the lines of compromise, if
not outright demands. Yes, a boyfriend was definitely in
order. She folded her arms again.

"Yes, as a matter of fact I do have a boyfriend."

Chuck knocked his index finger against the edge of his
desk. "Well, work will just have to take precedence. If he
doesn't know that already, he'll just have to learn."

"Agreed."

"Then you'll cancel your plans."

"Ah, no."

"Jenkins," he said sternly, "this is your job. I want you
at that dinner Friday night!"

She grabbed at the proverbial straw. "Dinner! Well, dinner, yes, I can probably swing that. I'll just, uh…"

Chuck's eyes narrowed, lending him the air of a truculent pig, but Denise was well aware that it would be unwise
to underestimate him. "Bring him along?" he suggested
smoothly, and the hair on the back of her neck stood up.

She had not the faintest idea what he was planning, but
no doubt he had something up his sleeve. The Chuck she
knew didn't take kindly to being thwarted in anything. She
gulped, trying to cudgel her reluctant brain into giving her
a solution, while Chuck warmed to his own scheme.

"By all means, bring him along! It'll be a pleasure to meet him. I insist. Really."

She felt like a rat trapped on a sinking ship, but if she had to choose, she'd just as soon go down with the ship as have to put herself into Chuck's hands in order to escape it. Coolly, she inclined her head in acceptance of his "invitation." It was only after she'd left his office some minutes later that she realized her little plan had one glaring flaw.

She didn't have a date on Friday, let alone a boyfriend.

It was, of course, the obvious solution, not so much because they were friends but because, more pointedly, he was the only single man she knew in the whole area! Moreover, something told her that he would not let her down. She could count on Morgan Holt to come to the rescue, but could she count on him not to take advantage or misconstrue? That was another question entirely. Yet she effectively had no choice. She needed a date for Friday night, a pretend boyfriend, and Morgan Holt was the only candidate. Quaking inwardly, she cleared her throat, inhaled deeply through her nose and shook her limbs, much as if she were preparing for a big match or an especially unnerving sales presentation. The small ritual behind her, she lifted her hand and knocked on the door.

A male voice called faintly from a distance through the door that he was coming. Denise folded her arms and stepped back, looking around the wide porch with its gingerbread trimming and fresh white paint contrasting with the pale sky blue of the house itself. It was really a lovely old home, not at all what she'd have picked out for herself but very much Morgan Holt. Somehow she sensed the love and pride that had gone into every brush stroke and swing of the hammer. He must have worked for years to refurbish the place. The elegant mahogany door with its large oval of beveled glass swung inward, and Denise jerked around, pasting a smile on her face.

"Hey! Good to see you. Come on in!" Morgan backed away from the door and allowed her to step past. "Man, it's beautiful out there, isn't it?" He inhaled deeply as he pushed the door closed. "I love this time of year. The leaves will start turning soon. Meanwhile the days are perfect and the nights are cool enough for a fire. What more could you want?"

"Nothing!" She tossed up her hands in a frivolous gesture so unlike her that she immediately regretted it. Morgan composed his squarely chiseled face and lifted a hand to indicate the first room immediately off the hall.

"Let's sit down, and you can tell me what's wrong."

Denise closed her eyes briefly, then opened them again and nodded at the same time as she looked around her. The hall was all polished wood and brass and sweeping stairs with marble treads and banisters. A large mirror, framed in heavy, ornately carved wood, hung on one wall, an old-fashioned hall tree stood opposite it. Between them a small, graceful chandelier hung from the ceiling, its brass inlaid with delicate cameos.

She followed Morgan into the living room. He put her on the couch and sat down opposite her on a wing chair, pulling it close and leaning forward with forearms braced against his knees. She crossed her ankles demurely and folded her hands in her lap, her heart beating a heavy rhythm.

"Okay," he said, "now what's wrong?"

She put on a smile, her voice falsely bright. "Nothing's wrong. I just thought you might like to join me and some, uh, other people for dinner…Friday night."

"Friday night," he echoed thoughtfully.

"At the Ozark Springs Inn," she added hurriedly. "I know it's late notice, but I promised I'd bring an, er, a friend. Honestly, Morgan, I'd be so appreciative if you could manage—''

"Okay," he said. "Now what's the rest of it?"

She was still hung on the *okay*. Breathless with relief, she sank back against the pillows and closed her eyes. "I can't tell you how much I appreciate—''

"Just tell me what's going on."

She sat upright again, suddenly believing that it was going to be all right, after all. "Actually," she said, almost laughing in her relief, "I don't need a date so much as I need a boyfriend. Oh, not that I want one, you understand! It's just that, well, my boss is a throwback to a less enlightened age, to put it politely. In fact, if I was willing to give up my career, I could nail him on sexual harassment charges. But I figure the best justice would be to get promoted despite him, maybe over him, and then don't think I wouldn't can his— Well, you get my meaning, I'm sure.''

She chuckled, expecting him to join her. He didn't. Instead he said, "I take it your boss will be joining us for dinner."

"Yes, and thank God that's all! He had the brass to try to pull off an overnight stay at the inn, which is why I told him that I already had plans."

"Uh-huh, and whose idea was the boyfriend?"

"His, actually. He just sort of jumped to that conclusion, and I let him think I had one in hopes it would make him think twice about planning any more overnight jaunts. Then he insisted that I bring you along for dinner. I mean, the boyfriend, not you necessarily. It's just that I don't know anyone else around here that I could ask to pretend with me. You do understand?''

He smiled then, but rather perfunctorily. "Sure. No problem."

She sighed, a hand pressed to her chest. "I don't know how to thank you."

"Hey, it's no biggie. I like the Ozark Springs Inn."

"Oh, good. I've never been myself, but now I can look forward to it. Oh, I should tell you that it's primarily a business dinner. We've brought on a new retailer, and the company rep will be there with us."

Morgan nodded thoughtfully. "That's fine. Is it just the four of us then?"

She pulled a face. "Chuck apparently doesn't bring his wife along to these things. Uh, Chuck, that's my boss."

Morgan nodded again. "Makes sense. No doubt having the little wife along would cramp his style."

"No doubt," Denise agreed drily. "One more thing. I think Chuck's planning something. When he insisted I bring along this fictitious boyfriend, he had a certain gleam in his eye, like he's got an ace up his sleeve. Don't be surprised if he does or says something outrageous."

"Something that would make a real boyfriend walk out maybe?" Morgan asked thoughtfully.

Denise nodded with satisfaction. "That would be my best guess."

Morgan shrugged. "No problem."

"You're sure?"

"I understand sharks like Chuck. Trust me."

Oddly, she did. "I can't thank you enough for this. I'll be eternally grateful."

"Hey, what are friends for?" Straightening, he rubbed his hands together in that exuberant way of his. "Now, can I get you a drink?"

"Oh, no, thank you. I don't drink much beyond a glass of wine with my dinner. It just seems to go straight to my head."

"Ah, you're wise to avoid it then."

"Yes, well, I'd better go," she said, growing uncomfortable again. "Smithson will be wanting his dinner."

"Speaking of dinner," he said, coming to his feet at the

same instant she did, "what time Friday should I be ready?"

"I don't really know. The reservations are for seven-thirty, but as I've never been to the inn, I can't say how long it will take us to get there."

"It's quite a drive," he said, "about forty minutes. How about if I pick you up around a quarter to seven?"

"Oh, you don't have to pick me up."

"Nonsense. I'm your date, remember. How would it look if your boyfriend just met you there?"

"Yes, I guess that wouldn't make quite the right impression. We can take my car, if you like."

"Nah, I'll just back the old Mercedes out of the garage. It doesn't get much use anymore. The drive will do it good."

"All right, if you're sure."

"My pleasure."

She turned and walked into the entry hall, saying, "You've been out to the Inn. What should I wear? Would a cocktail dress be too much?"

"No, I don't think so. I assume half the purpose of this dinner is to impress the new client, so to speak."

"Right. Well, then, I'll see you Friday."

"Friday," he said, opening the door for her.

She strolled out onto the porch. Dusk was already deepening into night. The smell of wood smoke permeated the chill. "Your home is lovely," she told him in parting.

"Thanks." He leaned a shoulder against the door frame and slid his hands into his pockets watching her as she descended the stairs to the walkway.

She sent him a last smile and hurried toward her apartment, wondering why her heart was again beating with such quick intensity. But this was not dread. This was... Dare she call it anticipation? And why not? Something told her that she'd just checkmated old Chuck, and come Friday, he'd know it. She was humming when she let herself into the apartment. She hummed all the way to Friday.

She opened the door to a kind of casual elegance she'd seldom seen in a man, and for a moment it held her spellbound. Perhaps it was the simplicity of a pale gray crewneck sweater worn beneath a gray silk jacket above classic black, pleated trousers. Or perhaps what held her spellbound was the way the grays shamelessly brought out the silver at his temples and the electric blue of his eyes; or maybe it was the slightly tousled look of his hair, worn short and sleek and sharply tailored, except in the very front, where it parted uncertainly in the middle and fell in two curving locks to his eyebrows. He looked relaxed and, at the same time, groomed within an inch of his life and utterly, totally male.

She didn't know how long she might have stood there and stared if he hadn't done a slow once-over, taken a step back and exclaimed, "Wow!"

She felt her own perusal turned back at her and literally blushed. She really didn't want him to know how much time she had spent getting ready for this make-believe event, and yet she was glad that she hadn't played down her appearance. The little red crepe slip dress with its gently flared skirt that swirled softly several inches above her knees was simple but classic. With spaghetti straps, it was a little light for a cool autumn evening, but she had augmented it with a long, clingy wrap of red organza, which at the moment was draped loosely about her shoulders and arms, hanging down almost to the tops of her red velvet heels and calling attention, she hoped, to slender ankles encased in the sheerest of black stockings. She hadn't known quite what to do with her hair, whether to wear it down or rolled into a classic French twist. In the end, she'd settled for something in between, a loose chignon pinned at the crown of her head with lots of long tendrils floating down around her face and shoulders. Her only jewelry consisted of pearl drops at her earlobes, a teensy gold chain about her throat and a pearl and rhinestone brooch that she wore pinned in her hair.

Apparently she had done well. Perhaps she had even overdone it. Morgan certainly seemed to find her appearance more than merely acceptable, and, for some reason, that sent a thrill down the back of her neck all the way to her toes. At least she hadn't outdone him, and to let him know that she fully appreciated that fact, she said to him, "You look wonderful!" at the same exact moment that he said it to her. Then they both laughed and said, "Thank you."

More laughter followed, and then he said, "Frankly, I was afraid you'd look all buttoned down the way you do when you leave for work in the mornings, not that you don't look good then, too, but, well, it wouldn't aid the illusion, so to speak."

"The illusion?"

"Of a woman in love," he said, leaning forward slightly. "You have a boyfriend, remember, not just a racquetball buddy—speaking of which, I think I deserve a rematch. I gave you a darn good game, if you'll recall."

She smiled, glad to have a "friendly" topic to discuss. "So you did. Give me another one tonight, and you're on."

"It's a done deal," he assured her as she gathered up her tiny, red velvet handbag. Stepping aside, he allowed her to move past him and out into the cool night. While she adjusted her wrap, covering her head and looping the ends just so about her shoulders, he locked the door and pushed it closed. Smithson jumped up into the window as they walked past, yowling as if he thought it was expected of him, then settling down to groom himself with leisurely strokes of his tongue. Likewise, Reiver woofed from his station on the porch.

"That's his protective post," Morgan informed her. "He always stations himself there when I'm gone."

"I've noticed that," Denise told him, and then wondered if she should have, but he seemed to find nothing remarkable about her taking note of his comings and goings. He talked on about the dog.

"It's part of his nature," Morgan said. "He'll stay right there until I get home and let him into the house for the night."

"He sleeps in your house?"

"Right in front of my son's bedroom door. It's as if he knows instinctively what means most to me and seeks to protect that."

"I've never seen your son. Does he get to visit often."

"Radley's up here all the time. You just probably didn't realize who he was."

"He lives close then?"

"He's a sophomore at the University of Arkansas in Fayetteville. Still."

"Still?"

Morgan chuckled. "Rad's not real serious about his course work. He's twenty already, and his mother thinks he's studying to be a bum just because he doesn't know yet what he wants to do. Hell, I didn't know what I wanted to do until I was thirty-eight."

They had reached the polished black automobile sitting in front of the old carriage house at the edge of the property. "And just what is it exactly that you are doing?" she asked as he opened the passenger door for her.

He laughed again, easily, lightly. "Whatever I damned well please. Currently that means remodeling an old house up on Hanson Creek for resale."

"Ah."

He handed her into the car, then bent over her, hands braced on the door frame and the door itself. "It doesn't compute for you, does it? I'll bet you made a five-year plan and stuck to it every step of the way.''

She didn't quite know what to say to that, for he was right, of course. Finally she asked, ''Is that bad?''

He shook his head. ''Nope. Unless you think it's the only way to live and expect everyone else to think so, too.''

She digested that while he came around and got in behind the steering wheel. Okay, maybe she had been pretty sure that it was the only way she could get what she wanted, and it had worked, so far as it went. So maybe she didn't quite understand why everyone else didn't do it, and maybe she had assumed that everyone just naturally wanted what she did. Was something wrong with that? Had she closed her mind to everything else? Her sister surely thought so. And perhaps her parents, now that she thought about it. But she was well into the second five-year plan, and everything was going along according to schedule, so why should she abandon her goals now? Of course she shouldn't.

On the other hand, when was the last time she'd really enjoyed herself? When had she last been happy? The answer to that lay buried back home in Kansas City, which meant, she reminded herself, that real happiness was forever out of her reach. What, after all, did she have left but her career? The answer was obvious, and yet it did not seem to have quite the bleakness about it that it usually did.

She didn't know whether to be alarmed or encouraged by that. She could never, would never, forget her son or the loss of him. So how could the knowledge that he was gone be any less shocking or sharp today than it had been yesterday? With that worrisome enigma on her mind, she almost missed the sight of Fayetteville spread like a swatch of stars in the Ozark foothills, down one eastern slope and into the flat valley below then north in a milky flow to

Springdale and Rogers and the cuts and gullies beyond. Thankfully, Morgan didn't let her miss it.

"This is one of my favorite sights," he said, jolting her from her reverie. "When I was a kid, I used to lie on my belly and look out the window of my attic room at the valley below and imagine what everyone in town was up to. It seemed another world even though we bused down every day to school."

"We?"

"My sister and I."

"I have a sister."

"Older or younger?"

"Younger."

"Me, too."

Something else they had in common. "I have a brother, too," she said, and felt a spurt of relief when he shook his head.

"I always wanted one, though."

Denise sighed as they turned back into the foothills and left Fayetteville behind. "So you lived up here, hmm?"

He nodded. "My dad's still up there. Delia—that's my sister—thinks he ought to move down to Little Rock with her, but he says he'll never leave my mom. She's buried up there near the house."

"Is it safe for him, so far from everything?"

He shrugged. "He says it is. Personally, I lived without indoor plumbing and electricity until I walked out of high school and into the University of Arkansas, and I didn't find anything particularly ennobling about it. But Dad says that life is best at its simplest, and frankly I see no reason for him to change his life now just because he's into his mid-seventies. He wouldn't be happy anywhere else."

"You must worry about him, though."

He inclined his head at that, saying, "I don't worry about much, frankly. If I see a problem and I can fix it, I do, but worrying never solved anything so far as I can tell.

Actually, as far as Dad goes, I admire him, and I always did, even when I was lost and so miserably unhappy I didn't know which way to turn.''

"And when was that?" she heard herself asking.

He considered a moment. "Oh, about ten years ago. That was the worst of it, anyway, though it had been building for a long, long time."

"And now?"

"Now I love my life," he said, grinning broadly. "I have everything I've ever wanted except…"

"Except," she prodded, and he turned his head to settle a look on her that was clearly meant to remind her that she had asked.

"Except someone to share it with," he said softly, and the yearning in his eyes made her turn away. She felt a bit sorry that she had asked, a little panicked, even, because something seemed to flutter in her chest when he looked at her like that, something she was too mature and too battered to feel, something that didn't belong in her second five-year plan, something that made her wonder if she had left out an important element. She pushed away the thought, fixing her mind on business, and she remembered what she had meant to tell him about Chuck, the warnings she ought to issue, the instructions she felt he needed to make this little charade work.

She spent the remainder of the drive doing just that, briefing him much as she would have a team going out on a major sales push. If he looked at her occasionally as if she secretly amused him, she let it pass without comment. After all, he was a friend doing her a favor, and a huge favor at that, not a subordinate questioning her judgment or instructions. He seemed to understand all that she had to tell him, commenting once that he knew Chuck's type all too well and another time that she shouldn't worry about the primary reason for the meeting—that being business—falling victim to the secondary reason, which he referred to as "nipping Chuck's extracurricular proclivities in the bud."

"I'll leave the former to you," he said. "Just you leave the latter to me."

She wasn't sure she liked the sound of that, but he reminded her of what she wanted to forget, specifically, that they were supposed to be in love or very close to it. He was right, of course. A casual date would do nothing to short-circuit Chuck's disgustingly sexual approach to her. A lover would—hopefully. The possibility existed that this would all be for nought. Chuck could be vicious enough to demand sexual concessions no matter what her personal situation, but her read on the situation was that he considered her fair game because she was unattached, so the obvious solution was to attach herself quickly to someone. And who else was there besides Morgan Holt? She was new to town, after all, and he had expressed an interest, but that was before he'd understood that she had no interest in anything more than friendship. Now that they understood each other, he'd proven a true friend, and that alone made him the appropriate candidate for this kind of date, not that this was a real date or anything. Certainly not. But it did feel oddly datelike even... She sat up a little straighter. Romantic? No, of course not! What could be romantic about pretending, about campaigning toward a goal? This was just another end run around the next fellow in her way. This was business. So what if the man with whom she'd chosen to align herself looked good enough to eat? So what if in an unguarded moment he made her heart beat a little faster? So what if the night was dark and soft and she felt cocooned in luxury and utterly feminine for the first time in so long that she couldn't remember ever feeling so, and the smile on his face and the appreciation in his eyes somehow caused a secret little thrill deep within her? So what?

So she was in trouble. That was what.

And, by golly, someone was going to pay. She narrowed her eyes, smiling when she imagined good old Chuck comparing himself to Morgan Holt and falling far, far short. Oh, yes, he was going to pay.

Chapter Three

Morgan pulled the Mercedes beneath the covered drive of the sprawling, rustic inn and rolled down the window. A white-jacketed valet wearing a small headphone bent forward and looked into the car. Morgan smiled. The Mercedes was eight years old, but the odometer had less than forty thousand miles on it, and the condition of the car was absolutely pristine. Morgan felt not the least desire to "trade up" to a newer model and wasn't sure that he ever would. The young valet returned his smile and swiveled down the tiny microphone suspended in front of his mouth.

"Do you have a reservation, sir?"

"We're meeting another party," Morgan said, deferring to Denise.

She leaned forward and looked at the valet. "A Mr. Charles Dayton."

The valet maneuvered the microphone back into position and spoke softly into it. "Mr. Charles Dayton." He pressed a fingertip to the speaker nestled inside his ear and his smiled broadened and warmed. He nodded to Morgan and Denise. "Mr. Dayton has arrived. Your names please."

They told him, and he relayed the message to whoever was on the other end of that microphone, then signaled to another valet, who quickly stepped up and opened the door for Denise, while the fellow with the mike did the same for Morgan.

Morgan strode around the car and caught up to Denise, who had already started up the steps. He slid his hand against the small of her back, pleased with the light, taut feel of her body, and leaned close to whisper into her ear. "Slow down. This is one battle that must be fought leisurely."

She slowed her stride, bowed her head slightly and nodded, slanting him a sly, grateful look that made his breath catch. If only she knew how loverlike he felt and how delighted he was that she'd given him this opening. Oh, his offer of friendship had been genuine enough, but only because he hadn't seen what else he could do. Even at that, he wouldn't have been surprised if she'd closed the door on him and his casserole. Instead, she'd let him inside and all but handed him the key to unlocking her so tightly buttoned-up self. He knew now that she had suffered great loss and hurt and because of it had closed off her emotional self, focusing all her energies on her career. Morgan knew from experience that a career could make a very poor partner with which to share a life, and he, for one, was more than ready to share his life with someone special. It was time for him. The question was, was it time for Denise? He knew that he was not going to look elsewhere until he found out. She drew him, this sleek, contained woman, and had done so since he'd first laid eyes on her.

The thickly timbered door of the lobby opened of its own volition as they approached, and another white-jacketed servant bowed them through, pointing as he did so toward a broad hallway on the right. Denise looked around her as they walked side by side through the expansive lobby with its warm aura of rusticity, taking in the massive beams, unglazed brick floors, and gargantuan, freestanding fireplace built of native rock and currently roaring with a small bonfire. The inn was famous for its homey luxury, mud baths and excellent food. It was perhaps infamous for its almost fanatically insured privacy, making it a favorite trysting place for well-heeled cheaters and the very, very discreet. Chuck had chosen his spot well. Fortunately Denise was too smart—and too upright—to be so easily caught in his web. Morgan knew that he was going to enjoy putting old Chuckles in his place, just as he enjoyed the knowledge that Denise was not nearly cynical enough or lost enough to sleep her way to the top. This was a woman of real substance.

Not for the first time, Morgan wondered what kind of idiot would toss such a woman aside, as her ex obviously had done—her and their child. The thought boggled the mind. How had a woman like Denise, who was obviously extremely sensitive, even gotten involved with a man like that? But then who was he to ask such a question? He, too, had loved the wrong person. He, too, had paid a heavy price. Ah, but life was good now. Still, it could be better. He thought of the nights he went to bed alone and of the mornings when only the company of his dog kept every day from beginning in a gray funk. His hand warmed against her back as he pictured Denise in his bed, tousled and soft, a smile spreading across her luscious mouth as she opened her eyes to find him there. Oh, yes, he was going to enjoy playing his part tonight—and hope that it inspired her to allow him to turn pretense into reality.

They strolled past various small, trendy shops and arrived at the entrance to the restaurant. They were greeted at once and led out into the maze of snowy white tablecloths and deep, comfortable chairs. Halfway across the room, Morgan slid his hand up to Denise's shoulder, feeling the satiny warmth of her bare skin beneath the filmy fabric of her wrap. "Denise."

She did just what he wanted her to do. She checked her graceful stride and craned her head back over her shoulder to look at him. He bent his head to hers and gave her a quick wink, whispering, "I just wanted to tell you again how very beautiful you are. Now smile. Just as though I really were your boyfriend."

She did so, blindingly, and it took no effort at all to put the appropriate amount of heat in his gaze as he smiled back. He settled his arm about her waist and urged her forward again. She was practically glued to his side when they reached Dayton's table. Both men immediately came to their feet. He knew which one was Chuck Dayton instantly. His smugness and not-quite-hidden irritation would have tipped Morgan off at any rate, but the covetous manner in which his gaze raked over Denise cinched it. Gerald Baker, in comparison, was a forthright, plainspoken gentleman.

"What a lovely young woman," he said baldly, "and bright as sunlight, too, I'm told. It's a pleasure to meet you, Ms. Jenkins."

"Why, thank you," Denise replied smoothly, then insisted that he call her by her given name as she lowered herself regally into the chair that Morgan held for her. She smiled up at him as she settled into place, and he let his gaze target her mouth, communicating his very real desire to kiss her, as much for her benefit as for Dayton's.

With the introductions made and the ice thoroughly broken, Morgan took his place at her side and immediately possessed himself of her hand, holding it lightly against his thigh. The small gesture did not escape Chuck Dayton, who had placed himself on Denise's other side at the small round table. Talk was trivial and sporadic as drink orders were taken and menus were presented. Then, as they waited for the appetizer to arrive, Chuck knocked back two bourbons and firmly steered the conversation to business matters.

Baker's company wanted to upgrade their merchandise as well as their image. He wanted recommendations concerning what brands should be dropped and which should be sought as replacements, as well as detailed cost analyses for each change, and he wanted Denise to handle the job personally. She quickly nailed down exactly what information he sought and in what format he preferred it and gave him a delivery date that seemed not only to please him but to surprise him, as well. Then she went on to tell him exactly what figures and reports she would need from him before she could start. He promised to fax her everything that she required first thing Monday morning. They quickly negotiated a consultation fee to be appended to the contract he had recently negotiated with another of Chuck's subordinates, and then Denise very coolly and very smoothly suggested that the fee might be waived if the contract, with its lucrative guarantee of minimum-order dollars, was extended to three years instead of one. It was obvious that the same idea had not occurred to Chuck and that it found great favor with both men. The deal was struck, and the business to which Chuck had wanted her to dedicate an entire night was concluded satisfactorily before the main course arrived.

Morgan placed a hand on her knee and squeezed lightly, smiling to let her know that he was both impressed and proud. He felt certain that the pleasure in her own replying gaze was genuine. Chuck ordered champagne to toast the moment, but Morgan carefully limited himself to a single glass. If Denise drank a little more deeply, well, Morgan didn't mind. He wouldn't object if she got a little bit tipsy, just enough to let down her guard and enjoy herself with him. Chuck, on the other hand, seemed to want to get her drunk. Every time she took so much as a sip from her glass, he was quick to replace it, so that it became difficult to gauge just how much she was actually imbibing. Morgan couldn't help wondering what he was up to, and then it became obvious.

Chuck began to touch her in an increasingly more intimate manner. First, he put on a good show of bonhomie and then just casually reached over and laid a hand over her forearm as he praised her competence. From there he progressed to clamping a hand over her shoulder, then patting and rubbing her back. He cupped her nape in the palm of his hand and eventually slung an arm around her shoulders. Long before he managed to work a kiss on the cheek into his routine, Morgan was struggling to maintain his calm, unconcerned facade. Only the sure knowledge that a reaction of jealousy was exactly what Dayton was after enabled Morgan to keep his cool. Denise was clearly uneasy with all the touchy feely stuff, but short of breaking his arm or dumping her wine in his lap, she was pretty much defenseless. The man was her boss, after all, and he was pawing her in front of an important client.

Worse, he was making it seem normal for the two of them, as if it was something that happened all the time. No doubt he wanted to plant doubts in Morgan's mind, foster the impression that he and Denise were already lovers. Morgan knew it was a lie and occasionally tried to telegraph Denise a message of support and reassurance while seeking a means of counteracting old Chuckie's shenanigans that would not reap untenable repercussions for Denise. When Baker's pager sent him from the table in search of a private telephone, Morgan knew the moment had arrived.

Using the moment of Gerald Baker's departure, Morgan leaned close to Denise and whispered that this was a good time for her to powder her nose. When she looked askance at him, he smiled and quietly implored her to trust him. She hesitated for perhaps five seconds, but then she calmly rose, excused herself, turned her back and gracefully strode away. He watched just until the door to the lounge swung

closed behind her. Then, without so much as a flicker of
warning, he reached across the table, grabbed Dayton's
expensive silk tie and hauled him forward, leaning in at
the same time in order to bring their faces nose to nose.

"Touch her again," he growled, "and I'll pulverize
your bones one by one."

The threat was out, and he was lightly patting Dayton's
cheek before the other man recovered enough to even think
of resisting, at which point Morgan merely released his tie
and leaned back. Crossing his legs, he smoothed the napkin
in his lap and smiled.

"I'm quite serious, you know," he said, ignoring Dayton's sputters. He locked his gaze with the other man's and
said clearly, "Try to use your position to coerce or seduce
her and I'll see you in hell if I have to take you there
personally. Do you understand me?"

Dayton started to reply, but Morgan shifted his gaze
away, caught sight of Gerald Baker making his way back
to the table and smiled in greeting.

"Do you understand?" he repeated just a tad more
forcefully through his smile, and a quick glance in Dayton's direction prompted a truculent nod. "Excellent. I
knew I could speak your language."

"Listen, smart guy," Dayton snarled, "you've forgotten
just one thing. What if she's the one who wants it?"

Morgan put his head back and laughed. Gerald Baker
was there before Dayton could do more than shut his gap-
ing mouth. "Oh, that's a good one," Morgan chortled, just
as Baker reached the table.

"Good joke?" Baker inquired, reclaiming his chair.

Morgan waved a hand. "You had to be here."

Gerald nodded, obviously eager to speak of something
else. "That was my wife. It looks as though I'll be a grandfather by morning!"

Morgan reached across the table to clap the older man
on the shoulder. "Congratulations! Your first?"

"Yes."

"Oh, that's wonderful. I hope everything goes well."

"It's looking good. Her mother didn't have a problem with any of ours."

"How many children do you have?"

"Four. Our youngest is still in high school."

"I have a twenty-year-old son."

They chatted on amicably, ignoring Dayton, for several moments before Denise returned to the table and Morgan recounted for her Baker's happy news. Denise exclaimed politely, and Morgan insisted on ordering dessert in celebration. Chuck insisted that another drink was in order and demanded more champagne. In comparison to everyone else's, his mood was positively morose, but he did manage some appropriate comments and even a few enthusiastic bites of the rich raspberry torte floated in whipped cream and drizzled with chocolate, but he didn't so much as allow his shoulder to brush Denise's as he nursed his wine.

Morgan, on the other hand, took advantage of the situation shamelessly. As it became more and more evident that Dayton had backed off, Denise became more and more relaxed, and Morgan himself refilled her glass. He then leaned close and eventually availed himself of her hand, receiving a warm squeeze in return. As the conversation became increasingly lighthearted, he put his arm around her. To his delight, Denise leaned into him, and once, in response to his praise of her racquetball game, even turned her head and placed a light, affectionate kiss at the corner of his mouth. By the time the prolonged dinner came to its inevitable end, it was obvious that Chuck had been quite effectively cowed and everyone else was well pleased, albeit for different reasons.

The group broke up amicably. Chuck went off silently in the direction of the front desk, while Gerald professed his desire to retreat to his room so he could call his wife on the telephone again. Denise and Morgan wished the new addition to the Baker family well and walked out arm in arm to find the valet already bringing the car around. Morgan reserved the privilege of handing Denise into the car for himself, tipped the valet lavishly and took the wheel. For his money, the evening had turned out extremely well, even if nothing else came of it. Still, now more than ever, he hoped, he prayed, that this was just a beginning of things to come.

Denise snuggled into the corner of her seat and laid her head against the headrest, sighing contentedly. She was happy and more than a little tipsy. And why not? She'd made a killer deal tonight, dinner had been marvelous, and her decision to have Morgan in on the evening had paid off handsomely. She couldn't help smiling when she thought of the changed Chuck she'd found, upon her return from the ladies' room. He had looked not only deflated but confused and even a little frightened. Whatever Morgan had said or done had achieved its objective, and she need not worry about retaliation due to the coup she'd single-handedly achieved with Baker. Chuck wouldn't dare give her a poor review after that bit of inspired negotiation. Oh, yes, she had been brilliant tonight—and she wasn't the only one.

Curiosity suddenly intense, she lifted her head and focused her gaze on Morgan's handsome profile. Heavens, he was a lovely sight. He looked every bit as delicious as she felt. She was glad that she'd chosen him. Indeed, she'd been proud to have him at her side. If she were in the market for a significant other, Morgan was just the sort of man she'd want. That thought, however, was too troubling to ponder for long, so she shoved it aside in favor of a less threatening one.

"Okay," she said, giggling, "how'ja do it?"

"Do what?"

She meant to figuratively "blow off" his feigned ignorance by puffing her lips and expelling a short burst of air through them. Instead, she blew a raspberry and had to clap her hand over her mouth to stop. They both laughed, and he said indulgently, "You seem to be feeling pretty good right now."

She wagged a finger at him unsteadily. "Don't change the shubject."

"What shubject?"

Had she really slurred her words? She supposed she had. She sat up a little straighter and said carefully, "What happened with Chuck tonight?"

He shrugged and concentrated on his driving. "We had a little talk, man-to-man, that's all."

She lifted an eyebrow at that, pretty certain what he meant. "You threatened him, huh?"

For a long moment he seemed not to even have heard her, but then he flashed her a smile that came in somewhere between delight and apology and said, "All right, yes, I threatened him. But it worked, didn't it?"

She laughed gleefully. "I'll say. You figuratively cut off his hands!"

"I had to do something," he teased, "considering the way you kept looking at your steak knife."

She laughed some more at that, feeling wonderfully carefree. How long had it been since she'd felt like this? She thought of Jeremy, and some of the delight in the moment waned, but somehow the automatic guilt trip did not kick in. Instead, she found herself thinking that it had been long before Jeremy was even conceived that she had last felt like this, long before ambition and drive had dominated her life, all the way back to childhood when good grades meant only an approving pat on the head, and summers were meant to be lazy and unfocused. She sighed, wondering when it had all changed. In retrospect, it seemed that one day she had been a happy-go-lucky child and the next she had been worried about getting into the best col-

leges after high school. One day she had been worrying
about what movie to see on Saturday night, and the next
she was consumed with her performance on the SAT.

Her carefree days had been long gone by college. She'd
known, of course, that a lot of the young people around
her had gone nuts, drunk on freedom, trying every new
thing that came along and studying only when no other
alternative could be found. But she had looked down her
nose at those people and concentrated on getting a 4.0 so
she could go into business school for her MBA. When
she'd made it, she remembered thinking that she could
lighten up some finally, but Derek had disabused her of
that notion.

She hadn't dated during college even casually, choosing
instead to concentrate on school. So she'd felt that she
owed it to herself to respond when Derek had first shown
an interest in her. She wondered now if she would have
fallen so completely for him if she hadn't been starved for
male attention. Unconsciously she had put aside feminine
things back in high school when she'd attacked her goals
with single-minded determination. When Derek had come
along, she'd been startled to find that feeling like a woman
was something she had never experienced, so it was no
wonder, really, that she'd latched on to him. He had been
more than willing. Why not? She had been ready to love,
and he had been ready to be loved. They'd met during the
first semester of graduate school, and their plans were laid
by the next. It wasn't until she had accidentally become
pregnant with Jeremy that she realized the entire relationship was based solely on her slavish devotion to Derek and
everything he wanted or espoused. The painful truth was
that Derek had never loved her, and when he and his goals
had stopped being the complete focus of her attention, he
had walked away as easily as he changed his socks, leaving
her alone to support and parent a helpless child. There had
been no carefree moments after that—until tonight.

She closed her eyes and savored the moment, unwilling to even acknowledge how fleeting it would undoubtedly be. Instead, she smiled at the vision that shimmered before her mind's eye, Chuck sitting politely silent like the gentleman he was not, while Morgan's arm encircled her protectively. She searched her mind for something with which to compare that moment, but none came to mind. She had felt protected in her father's arms as a child, but that was only a part of what she had felt tonight. Tonight she had felt not only protected but valued for all that she was—and more. She had felt incredibly sexy. She had felt protected, accomplished, adult, and very feminine. They were all things she had felt before, of course, but never all at once. It was a heady combination, especially when augmented by fine wine, and she admitted to herself now that it could be addictive, as well. The fact that she did not yet want to give it up was proof of that.

She didn't know how long she floated there in that moment of memory, but gradually she became aware of something outside the moment. It was nothing more than a niggling sense of irritation at first, but gradually it coalesced into a hand determinedly shaking her and a voice that would not go away.

"Come on, babe. Time to go inside. Wake up. Wake up now, sweetheart. Come on. Time to wake up."

Sighing, she opened her eyes, but nothing immediately happened. Several seconds passed before her eyes focused on a shape somehow more intense than the darkness around it. She sat up straight and rolled her head to alleviate a slight stiffness in her neck. "Where are we?"

"In my garage. Here let me help you with that." The voice in her ear was no longer irritating but silky and warm. He reached a hand around to the nape of her neck and began to massage the muscles there. For several delightful minutes he worked magic on her muscles. "Good?"

"Wonderful." She moaned with a pleasure so luxurious it bordered on sinful.

"Then I'll just keep it up." He added the strength of his other hand, saying, "Let me know when you want to go in."

She mumbled that nothing had ever felt so good. His hands stopped, and he bent his head close to hers as if to hear her better.

"Do you want to go in?"

She shook her head. She didn't want to go anywhere. Here was the loveliest place she'd been in a long, long time.

"Okay." His voice now seemed laden with promise. It made her shiver with anticipation. "But I have to warn you," it went on. "If we sit here much longer, I'm going to have to kiss you."

Her lungs stopped working, her breath trapped in her chest. Kissing. She tried to think when she had last been kissed and flashed on the day of her wedding to Derek, but something told her that this would be nothing like that cool, practiced, showy meeting of lips. Something told her this would be unlike anything she had ever before experienced. In the darkness she could almost make out his features, not that she really needed to see him. Morgan Holt filled her every sense, his image permanently emblazoned on her memory's viewfinder. Oriented by the faint silvering at his temples, she focused on his mouth and waited for it to happen. To her frustration, he took his time.

His hands went still at the back of her neck. Then, slowly, one hand lifted to brush her cheek lightly and finger a strand of hair wafting about her face before traveling to her shoulder and pulling her forward slightly, so that the hand at her nape could slip down and around, coming to rest at her side beneath her arm and several inches above her waist. Once positioned, he simply folded her close and put her face next to hers. He probed gently with his nose, nuzzling and teasing, until his mouth brushed hers and finally, oh, finally, settled into place.

For a long moment out of time, his mouth held hers in thrall. And then someone moaned. Whether it was him or her hardly seemed to matter, only that it proved the catalyst to something far deeper and stirring, something that caused him to slide his arms fully about her and pull her tightly against his chest, his mouth widening hers, opening her for the thrust of his tongue and the scalding, searing ignition of pure desire.

Suddenly she was needy. Every pore and cell yearned for skin against skin, for hands that molded and smoothed, for the sharp edges of teeth that ground against her own, and the probing, stroking, filling stab of a moist tongue. Desperately she pushed her arms up and wrapped them tightly around his neck, pressing herself against him. She needed a male counterpoint, hardness where she was soft, heat where she was cold, certainty where she was unsure, and she needed it inside, battering, pounding, demanding for entry and jointure. She needed sex, hot, mindless, elemental, and she needed it with him, with Morgan, only Morgan. And the very thought of it scared her sober.

She jerked back, wrenching her mouth from his and gasping for breath. The sharp physical need did not abate. Frantically she grappled with the door handle and nearly tumbled out of the car when the door swung open. If not for his hands on her body, she would have. Yet, he did not hold her when she struggled for release.

"Denise, wait!"

"No!" She swung her feet out and literally jumped, staggering as she rose.

"Be careful! Damn!"

Her head swam, and she grabbed for something to steady her. Her palm grazed the wall, and she flattened herself against it. She hadn't even caught her breath when strong hands seized her and turned her around.

"Are you all right?"

She couldn't swallow, let alone speak, and she was freezing for some reason. She was freezing and he was warm. Gratefully, frantically, she pressed against him, aware that her actions made no sense, that she was asking him to protect her against himself. He locked his arms around her, crooning soothingly.

"It's all right, honey. It's all right. You've just had too much to drink. I won't take advantage of that again, I promise. Come on. Let's get you inside."

She nodded and allowed him to carefully tuck her wrap about her, her hands clutching his lapels. Just the caring, gentle movements of his hands woke in her needs she had thought long buried, to be cared for, to be wanted. The thought floated through her mind that tomorrow would be too late, for some reason. This was the only moment of cosseting and treasuring that she would have. Panicked, she whispered his name, and without even meaning to, without even knowing that she was going to do it, she pressed her mouth to his again.

He, too, seemed to sense that it was the only moment they would be allowed, for he tightened his arms about her and quite thoroughly tasted and explored her mouth. He pressed her back against the wall, fitting his body to hers, skimming her with his hands from face to thighs and upward again to her breasts, cupping and lifting them, while his hips held her in place and his mouth mated with hers. Ah, heaven. Had she ever felt this good? Had she ever wanted a man's hands on her more? His breath came in hard pants, while hers seemed caught forever in her chest, making her head swim and her heart hammer. He moved against her, rocking his hips, and the need flared so hot that she keened with it, breaking her mouth from his and turning up her face. He skimmed kisses along her jaw to the hollow behind her ear and went very still. His hot breath painted her skin. Slowly, carefully, he began to move away, his body easing back, hands sliding to her waist. Finally, he lifted his head.

Sweet, clean breath filled her lungs. She was torn between relief and disappointment, between shoving him away and pulling him close once again. She could do neither. Weakly, she began to tremble with very real cold and opened her eyes to find him staring down at her. He took his hands away and pushed them through his hair, one after the other, breathing deeply.

"I knew it," he said to no one in particular. "I just knew it."

She wanted to ask what he knew, but suddenly she was just too tired, too drained. Her teeth chattered. He laid a hand on her shoulder and pulled her easily away from the wall.

"Come on, sweetheart. Let's get you inside. The temperature's dropping like a rock in a well." He stepped to her side and wrapped a bracing arm about her waist.

Resigned to doing as she was told, she laid her head on his shoulder and allowed him to usher her through a side door and out into the night. He wasn't kidding about it getting cold. It seemed to batter her with tiny pinpricks of icy discomfort, or was that sleet? She shivered, and he wrapped both arms around her, hurrying her across the ground. She bowed her head to keep the ice from stinging her face. When they stopped and she looked up again, they were standing at her door. He slipped her tiny purse from his jacket pocket and opened it. Finding her keys, he extracted them, pushed the purse beneath his arm and opened the door.

He practically lifted her over the threshold and closed the door behind them. Smithson darted between their feet, but when Denise looked down she couldn't find him. Morgan seemed uninterested in returning the greeting her cat had given them. Denise frowned. She always returned Smithson's welcome. It was the only one she ever received. She thought of telling Morgan that, but her tongue simply wasn't working and he was hustling her through the apartment so quickly that it took all her strength just to stay on her feet.

Before she knew what was happening to her, they were standing in her bedroom, and Morgan was slipping her wrap off her shoulders. Quickly, he turned her, and she felt his hands in the center of her back. Then suddenly his hands were at her shoulders and her dress was sliding down her body to the floor, pooling at her feet. She swayed gently, aware that she was standing before him in nothing more than a strapless teddy, her shoes and sheer black stockings. Her hands moved uneasily over her body, as if hunting for something that needed shielding and finding nothing actually exposed. Oh, well. It was too late now at any rate.

He shoved her down on the edge of the bed and knelt beside her, lifting her feet one by one to skim off her shoes. Then he pulled back the covers and pushed her down against the pillow, lifting her feet and tucking them away. The covers folded over her, surrounding her in soft warmth. She sighed as he tucked them beneath her chin. He turned away, bending to pick up her dress and drape it over his arm. For some reason that seemed an especially sweet thing to do. She made up her mind to tell him so.

"Morgan."

"Hmm?"

But she had already forgotten what she wanted to say. She rolled onto her side and sighed. Her eyes drifted shut. "Jus', Morgan."

Something feathered across her temple, and then her hair tumbled down around her face. Darkness slid over her, and with it, sleep. Consciousness spun away, until all that was left was his mouth on hers, his hands skimming her body, and an unanswered need throbbing deep inside her. Morgan.

Morgan.

Chapter Four

Moaning, Denise let her head fall forward, catching it in both hands just to be certain that it didn't fall off. What on earth was wrong with her? The only other time in her life when she'd had too much to drink was at her wedding. As a result, she remembered hardly anything at all about her wedding night, a fact she no longer regretted. Unfortunately, she feared that she'd forgotten nothing about last night. Truthfully, she remembered only too well. She seemed to have relived that kiss over and over in her dreams all night long. So vivid had the memories been that she had awakened this morning expecting to find Morgan there, and only the pain in her head had felt sharper than her disappointment when she realized that he was not. That in itself was enough reason never to see him again. The fact that he'd caused her to get drunk, she told herself stubbornly, was another.

She'd conveniently forgotten how very nervous she had been in the early part of the evening, and how her glass had never seemed to empty. She chose not to recall that it had been Chuck buying the drinks early on, or that she had taken specific note of the fact that Morgan was not drinking and had decided that she could, therefore, afford to indulge just a bit. The stark facts were that she had had too much to drink, and Morgan had taken advantage of that.

Friendship, obviously, was no longer a possibility between the two of them. They, *he,* had stepped over the line last night when he'd kissed her. If she'd kissed him back, well, she had the alcohol to thank for that. It certainly wasn't because she was ready to let another man into her life. She wasn't sure that she'd ever be ready for that. Her career took center stage for now and the foreseeable future. That's what last night had been about, after all—business, not romance. Morgan had ignored a promise to keep things light between them. He had turned a favor between friends into seduction. Well, she wouldn't let herself believe that he was harmless again. She would darn well keep her distance from now on.

Smithson meowed and rubbed insistently against her ankles, demanding breakfast. Denise frowned, but she got up and shuffled over to the pantry for the cat food. Bending over to fill the dish was an indescribable agony, but Smithson was grateful enough to rub her ankles again, purring, before attacking the food. Denise leaned over the counter and laid her cheek against the cool top, waiting for the aspirin she'd taken earlier to go to work. When the doorbell rang, she moaned and covered her head with her arms, the sound lancing through her skull like white lightning.

The bell chimed again before she could make her way through the dining and living area to the small entry and the door. Consequently, she was scowling when she pushed open the door to find Morgan's smiling, handsome face.

"What?"

He blinked at the sharpness of her tone, then smiled apologetically and lifted a white paper sack. "Thought you might be able to use some coffee and a Danish about now."

"No, thanks," she said curtly and yanked the door closed. Guilt immediately swamped her, and she was reaching reluctantly for the doorknob again when it turned and the door opened seemingly of its own volition.

He thrust the paper bag at her, saying, "You might as well take this. I hate to waste my money, especially after I've wasted so much of my time."

The bag dropped toward the floor. Gasping, Denise managed to catch it, but when she looked up again, the door was closing in her face this time.

On Monday morning Denise strode toward the office door, smiling as Betty rose from her desk. "Do you have something for me, Betty?"

"Mr. Dayton wants you in his office first thing."

Denise sighed and glanced at her wristwatch. Nodding briskly, she pushed through her office door and went straight to the desk, where she placed her handbag in a bottom drawer before picking up the file she'd carried in and leaving with it. She paused once more at her secretary's desk.

"This may take a while. If my eight-thirty gets here before I get back, ask him to wait, then let me know. All right?"

"Yes, ma'am."

"You know where to reach me." With that she strode off in the direction of Chuck's office.

When she got there, she found the secretary's desk unoccupied and the door standing open. Shrugging, she walked through. Chuck wasn't at his desk. She turned toward the sitting area where he often entertained clients and bigwigs, just in time to see Chuck slide his hand up under his cute blond secretary's short skirt as she bent forward to pour him a cup of coffee. She giggled, the airhead, and he moved his hand under her skirt.

Denise tamped down her distaste and cleared her throat,

loudly. Little Miss Idiot straightened with a jerk, and Chuck snatched his hand back, turning a look over his shoulder. When he saw who it was, he relaxed and patted his secretary on the bottom reassuringly. It took all of Denise's self-control not to roll her eyes. Chuck signaled her over with a wave of his hand. Well, well, so she rated the sitting area now. Why didn't that make her feel better?

"Hey, how was your weekend?"

"Fine. And yours?"

"So-so." He patted his secretary again and said to her, "Pour Ms. Jenkins a cup, too, sweetie."

Sweetie gladly complied. Apparently she considered serving coffee while the boss mauled her a legitimate, perhaps even preferred, job description. When she was through, she set down the coffee decanter and quickly retreated, saying that she'd be right outside if they needed her. Chuck ignored her. Out of reach, out of mind.

He crossed his legs, fixing Denise with a benign gaze. "Do I have to tell you how high your stock's gone around here?"

"I never turn away praise."

He chuckled. "Okay, then maybe I ought to tell you that I called the Big Guy this morning." He meant the vice president of operations, his direct supervisor. "Baker had already beat me to it. Your name is now on the *A* list. If you weren't on the fast track before, you are now."

Smiling, Denise took a deep breath. She felt a good deal of satisfaction—but not the elation she had expected. She pushed that thought away and reached instead for her coffee cup, while Chuck talked about the possibilities suddenly available to her. She might think about concentrating on contract negotiations or tailored market studies. The implication was that a promotion of some type was imminent. Denise found herself listening with only one ear, her thoughts straying yet again to Morgan Holt.

As badly as she hated to admit it, a lot of the credit for

her latest coup went to Morgan. His support had allowed her to make the deal with Baker and kept her from becoming prey to Chuck's lascivious inclinations. She felt lousy about the way she'd treated him on Sunday morning, but she couldn't find any way to undo it without encouraging him. If only he hadn't kissed her. If only she hadn't kissed him back. She really would have liked to have had him as a friend. Chuck seemed to be reading her thoughts. His mention of Morgan's name snapped her back to full attention.

"Not that Morgan's exactly the type I'd have expected you to go for," Chuck was saying. "Sort of possessive, isn't he?"

Denise schooled her face into blandness. "Yes, I suppose you could say that."

"It doesn't bother you?"

She smiled secretively. "Not in the least."

"Jealous, is he?"

She fixed her gaze on his face. "Not without reason."

Chuck waggled his foot nervously. "Strikes me as the kind who could get real worked up."

"Does he?"

"Got a bad temper, I'd say."

She let a grin break out across her face. "And the muscle to back it up."

"You can handle that type, can you?"

"What do you think?"

He ignored that and said, "You've always struck me as the sort to put ambition first. This Morgan fellow doesn't seem to fit with that."

"Morgan knows how I feel about my career," she said flatly, her tone making it clear that said feelings were not negotiable.

"Hmm." He uncrossed his legs and changed the subject. "What do you want to do about the Anthony proposal?"

Denise reeled inwardly. Suddenly her opinions were

worth something? She actually had some say around here? Smoothly she sat forward, quickly marshaled her thoughts and said, "We don't want to give away the store on that one. I think we should just sit tight for a day or two. Let Baker pass the word around, then go back with a similar proposal."

He nodded and reached for his coffee cup. "Good thinking. You'd better nail the proposal yourself. I'll sound out Anthony and get back to you."

"Sounds good to me."

"Okay." Chuck leaned forward and clapped his hands together. "I don't have anything else just now. How about you?"

She started to shake her head, then a particularly thorny problem that she'd seen coming for some time popped into mind. Did she dare? And why not? It was well within her scope. She made an offhand gesture. "Actually, there is something. A member of our sales staff is pregnant."

Chuck made a face. "Hell. Maternity leave tears up a quota schedule."

"I'm aware of that."

"Find some way to get rid of her."

Denise pursed her lips, her heart beating like a kettle drum. "Actually, that could be trouble."

"How so?"

She decided on a self-deprecating approach. "Well, I could be way off base, but she strikes me as the sort to go straight to her lawyer. We could be looking at a discrimination suit. Now, I may be worrying over nothing, but I'd prefer not to take chances."

"So what do you propose we do?" he wanted to know. "Hold her hand during labor?"

Denise chuckled. "I was thinking more along the lines of transferring her to another department."

Clearly, so simple a solution had never occurred to

Chuck Dayton. His brows rose in tandem. "Can we do that?"

"I'm sure I can find some place for her."

"Will she take a transfer?"

Denise grinned. "I'll find a way to sell her on it. Even if we have to give her a small raise in salary to offset the loss of commission, we'll still come out way ahead. Just the cost of defending a lawsuit—"

Chuck waved a hand dismissively. "Sounds like you've got the situation in hand. Best get on with it. The sooner we transfer her the less likely she is to connect it with her little bun in the oven."

"My thoughts exactly." Trying hard not to smile, she got to her feet, glanced at her wristwatch and started toward the door, saying briskly, "I've got an appointment in five minutes. Have a good one."

"Yeah, you too." Just as her hand reached out for the brass knob on his door, he called out her name. "Hey, Denise?"

She froze, wondering if he might have changed his mind already, but no, he wouldn't have. Pasting a smile on her face, she turned. "Yes?"

He'd twisted around in his chair and was grinning at her like the cat who'd swallowed the canary. "I was just thinking that the two of us make a pretty good team, wouldn't you say?"

Relief, mingled with distaste, filled her. "A business partnership made in heaven," she lied smoothly, and then she got out of there before he could see the revulsion in her eyes. She had to remind herself why she was doing this. Not only had she saved an expectant mother's job, she'd headed off Chuck's amorous intentions, for now—for as long as she could keep him believing that Morgan Holt was the man in her life. As long as she could do that, her career was safe. But God help her if either one of them ever found out about this particularly convenient lie.

* * *

Morgan winked at the pretty attendant who wrote her own name in the space designated for the name of the member whose guest he was. She was entirely too young for his comfort, but he was willing to overlook that if doing so would help him get Denise Jenkins off his mind. If he had hopes of seeing her here at the gym this evening, he steadfastly refused to acknowledge them. Instead, he glanced over the racquetball court reservation list, looking for a likely partner. Chuck Dayton's name caught his eye, and he grinned when he saw that another man's name had been scratched out beside it. Flirting outrageously, he borrowed a pen from the attendant and wrote his own name over the one that had been scratched out. Then he winked at the perky blond and took himself off to stretch and warm up.

Chuck had not yet arrived when Morgan entered the closed-in court. Morgan was well aware that if Chuck's partner had notified him personally of the change in plans, Chuck might not even show up. Nevertheless, he began swatting a ball around in preparation for play. Three or four minutes later, Chuck lumbered into the room in his expensive warm-up suit and shoes, a sweat band encircling his bald head, a black leather bag in hand.

"Morgan! What are you doing here?"

Morgan caught the ball in one hand and turned to face Chuck. "Hoping to pick up a game. Your partner canceled. Or didn't you know?"

"Halstead canceled?" Chuck mumbled warily. "How did you know?"

"I read the list."

Chuck stared, no doubt thinking through the situation. Morgan recognized the instant when old Chuck convinced himself that he could beat Morgan and win back a little of his own. He nodded and said too heartily, "Good thing for me you were around to take his place."

Morgan inclined his head, grinning. "My pleasure."

Chuck dropped his bag and began stripping off his warm-ups. "I have to warn you, though, I don't like losing."

Morgan chuckled. "Who does?"

Chuck shrugged. "Don't say I didn't warn you. I always beat Denise, you know."

"Do you?"

"And I understand that Denise beat you."

"Where did you hear that?"

"Around the gym. You didn't let her win, did you?"

Morgan gave the ball a satisfying whack and said, "I never let anyone win."

Chuck seemed to take that as a guarantee of his own victory, for he laughed as he took out his racquet and set his other things outside the door. Morgan insisted that the older man take a few minutes to warm up. As he did so—stretching and jogging and wiggling in place, then slapping a ball around—he talked of Denise.

"Great head on that girl, not that the rest of her isn't top-notch, too."

"She isn't a girl," Morgan pointed out blandly.

Chuck chuckled. "Some of the guys in the office call her Dennis, but I always figured she was all woman, and you'd be the one to know, being her boyfriend."

Morgan gave him a quick look at that. Hadn't Denise told him that they were no longer an item, however imaginary? Or had the subject merely never come up again after their dinner together? He didn't ask, choosing to listen instead as Chuck rambled on.

"I have to say that I'm a little surprised, though."

"Why is that?"

"You don't seem the type, that's all."

Morgan gave him a full-face look. "What type would that be?"

''You know, the type to take a back seat to a woman's career.''

''Ah. And, um, did Denise say specifically that I was that type?''

Chuck shrugged and dropped into his stance. ''More or less.'' He signaled with a nod that Morgan should serve, and Morgan made ready to do so, pausing only a moment longer.

''And when did she do that?''

Chuck gave him a curious but offhanded glance before sliding his gaze back to the ball perched on Morgan's fingertips. ''She's always talking about you.''

Morgan nearly dropped the ball. ''Since we had dinner together, you mean?''

''Sure. I didn't know a thing about you before then. No one did.''

The little sneak! She was going around telling everyone that he was her guy—and after cutting him off at the knees like that! A sly, wicked grin narrowed his eyes. Oh, this was going to be good. This was going to be very good. He served the ball.

Distraction nearly cost him that first game, but he managed to relegate Denise and what he was going to demand of her to the back of his mind long enough to squeak by. Games two and three were handy wins, however, and by the end Chuck was just barely able to go through the motions, his face a doughy mass of blood red, his breath wheezing in and out. Morgan clapped him on the shoulder and declared facetiously that he was just having a bad day. Chuck was too winded to even make face-saving agreement. Morgan bounced into the shower and then dressed and combed his hair. When he came out again, Chuck was still trying to work up the energy to take off his shoes. Morgan wished him a merry farewell and went out whistling. He felt better than he'd felt since that night over two weeks ago when Denise had so ardently kissed him back.

The October wind was bracing enough to turn downright nippy when it flowed over his wet head, but he merely turned up the collar of his navy blue cardigan, hunched his shoulders and kept walking. Reaching the late-model, light blue truck that he drove every day, he got in and drove straight home. Less than ten seconds later, he was knocking on Denise Jenkins's door.

Denise stood at the end of the kitchen counter, one hand braced flat against its top, and bent forward, lifting first one foot and then the other to whisk off her shoes. It was heaven to stand flat-footed. She put her head back and luxuriated in the feel, listening to Smithson delicately crunching his cat food. Such a day! And to make matters worse, the temperature was dropping at an alarming rate. She shivered, dreaming of a long soak in a hot tub and knowing that instead she would be spending the evening curled up on the couch with a number of files to be studied. Sighing, she rolled her head side to side and bent to pick up her shoes. Just as she straightened, someone knocked at her door—someone she hoped was a complete stranger.

Warily she carried her shoes into the entry and looked at the door as if doing so would tell her who stood outside. Finally she leaned forward and peeked carefully through the spy hole. None other than Morgan Holt stood fidgeting on her doorstep. Denise closed her eyes, a sense of foreboding washing over her. For a long, tense moment she considered pretending that she wasn't home, but her car in the carport would give her away. Besides, she told herself, this didn't mean that he was on to her. He was her landlord, after all. She took a deep breath and reached out to flick open the door. As it swung outward, her gaze quickly took in the dark, snug jeans and loafers, worn with a burgundy turtleneck beneath a navy cardigan with big, wooden buttons, and wet hair. He stepped up into the entry without waiting for an invitation and pulled the door closed behind him.

"Chilly out there," he said, shivering.

She let her gaze whip over his wet hair. "Don't you have sense enough to dry your hair before you go out in weather like this?"

He shrugged. "I was in a hurry."

"Well, so am I," she replied dismissively. "I have work to do, so if you could make this brief, I'd appreciate it." She struck what she hoped was a nonchalant pose, despite the shoes clutched by the heels in one hand. He turned and took himself into her living room, again ignoring the fact that she hadn't invited him inside. Temper piqued, she went after him. "You are the rudest man!" she exclaimed. "I've already told you I don't have time for this! Now say what you have to say and go!"

He sat himself down on the sofa and got comfortable. Obviously he was going to take his own sweet time, the cad. Well, she'd be hanged if she'd play his game. She planted her feet and folded her arms, glaring him into speaking. When he did, she wished he hadn't.

"I saw Chuck at the gym today."

Denise felt the color drain from her face. Oh, God. Oh God oh God oh God. She swallowed the sudden lump in her throat and tried to think of a reply. She needn't have bothered. He displayed every intention of controlling the conversation.

"Actually," he said with terrible brightness, "we played a game of racquetball. I won, of course, and it was a real treat. You should try it some time, beating old Chuck—or just playing him fair and square."

Having regained a little of her aplomb, she forced a smile and sank down on the very edge of the armchair. "I, um, I would enjoy that. Unfortunately I'm an employee, and Chuck is the kind of boss who—"

"Expects to be allowed to win," he finished for her.

"Yes, I know. What a pity. Puts a person in a very difficult position. I imagine it's hard to maintain one's personal integrity in a situation like that. Why, a person might even resort to…schemes, falsehoods. Even outright lies."

Denise gulped, color returning to her face in a rush of hot red. Obviously he knew everything. It was no use pretending that he didn't. She took a deep breath, surprised at how close to tears she was. "Wh-what did you say to him?"

He stared for a long time, then dropped his gaze to a piece of lint on the arm of the sofa, his fingers flicking at it repeatedly. "Nothing. Too bad you can't say the same. Tell me, just what it is that you go around saying about me all the time? I mean, since you talk about me so much, not that couples don't discuss each other on occasion. It's just that we're not…a couple, that is. Except according to Chuck—and you, apparently." With that last he raised his gaze and nailed her to the chair.

Denise felt about as small as a flea, but she'd fought too hard and too long to give up without even making an attempt to defend herself. "I…I didn't exactly tell him that we're a couple. He just assumed it. Naturally, he would after—"

"Naturally. And naturally you never thought to inform him that you weren't even speaking to me, let alone…well, doing what couples do together."

She licked her lips. "I, um, didn't think you'd mind. After all, you agreed to pose as my boyfriend."

"So I did," he said affably, "and in return you slammed a door in my face."

"You kissed me!" she blurted.

"And you kissed me back."

"That's not the point! Friends don't kiss! Friends…"

"Pretend? That's all we were doing, Denise, pretending we didn't want to kiss. Besides, some people think of friendship as the starting point of a relationship, not the end of one.''

''You were just using friendship as a way to get close to me!'' she accused.

''Yes. And you were using me as a pawn in your little game of professional chess with old Chuck. It's true that I was perfectly willing—for the chance to get close to you. But you shut me out.''

She shook her head, not because she hadn't done it, but because he made it sound so...wrong. He just didn't understand that she couldn't, wouldn't, risk that kind of emotional involvement again. ''You shouldn't have kissed me,'' she said in a small voice that she barely recognized as her own.

''I disagree,'' he said calmly. ''I think you need to be kissed in the very worst way, and I refuse to apologize for wanting to be the one to do it. Next time—''

''There won't be a next time!'' she exclaimed, shooting up to her feet, her shoes forgotten in the chair behind her.

''Oh, I think there will be,'' he said. ''At least the opportunity for it...unless you've decided that honesty is the best policy, after all.''

She didn't miss his meaning. He was blackmailing her! He was threatening to tell Chuck that they were not a couple, but he was saying more than that, too. He was offering her his protection, providing... What? Surely he could see that forcing himself on her would make him every bit as unattractive as Chuck himself. Yes, of course he did. Her own instinct told her that this was not about sex or power for Morgan. What he wanted from her was infinitely more dangerous. This was about love. What he wanted from her was her love. But she couldn't give it. And suddenly she knew that was her protection from him, her inability to love again. Perhaps by the time he found out that about her, she would have slipped past Chuck on the career ladder. So what if he kissed her again. So what if she kissed him back. That would never be enough for Morgan Holt, and that would save her. She relaxed her hands, her fingers gradually uncurling. "What do I have to do?"

He spread his hands and said oh so innocently, "Nothing. Unless... Well, I do have this problem with my father."

"Your father?"

"Mmm, the problem, really, is my sister. She thinks we should put him in a nursing home, but I disagree. He's happiest where he is, and as long as his mind is good, which it is, I don't see that we even have the right to try to tell him where he should live. I was thinking that maybe you could give me your opinion. Not without seeing firsthand how he lives, of course, which you could do, say, Sunday afternoon? I usually visit him on Sunday afternoons. You could come along. If you want."

"Sunday afternoon?" she echoed pensively.

"I could really use another woman's perspective," he added needlessly. "What do you say?"

What could she say? She relaxed her stance and forced out the words. "Sunday afternoon...would be okay, I guess."

"Excellent." He got to his feet, smiling down at her as benignly as if he hadn't just coerced her into what amounted to a date. Well, let him smile, and let him keep on smiling until she had what she needed from him, and then... Well, then he'd have no one to blame but himself. She'd tried to make him understand. It wasn't her fault that he couldn't take no for an answer.

He stepped forward, and she stepped back, more from a sense of self-preservation than anything else. His smile became rather smugly knowing. "About two?" he asked.

She nodded briefly. "Fine. Now I really must get to work."

"All right." He headed toward the entry. "Then I'll see you Sunday."

"At two," she confirmed, following.

He gave her a last smile and went out the door. She closed it and leaned against it. Everything was going to be fine, she told herself. Morgan hadn't spoiled things with Chuck, and he wouldn't force her into a physical relationship. Seduce her, yes, but force her, no. And since she couldn't be seduced, well then, she had nothing to fear. This quaking inside was nothing more than embarrassment at being found out. Nothing more. Yes, everything would be fine. Just fine.

Morgan stood on the doorstep, hunched against the chill wind, and smiled to himself. She'd looked so cute standing there in her bare feet with her shoes in her hand. All the fight had gone out of him at the first sight of her, all the indignation disappearing like so much mist in the morning sun. But he wasn't fool enough not to use the tools she'd given him. He'd thought that it was over, that no avenue of approach was left to him. He'd just assumed that she'd changed her mind about passing him off as her boyfriend, that she'd rather fend off old touchy-feely Chuck than risk kissing him again. Now that he knew otherwise, he had a way to get next to her, and he'd be damned if he wouldn't use it.

Not that he'd really blow her story to Chuck. He was no more happy about the idea of Chuck touching her than he had been before. In fact, he'd intended to tell Chuck that the threat still stood, no matter that he and Denise had "broken up." That had been the main reason he'd gone to the gym today, but what Chuck had said to him had changed everything. He could only hope that something positive would come of this.

Just what it was about Denise Jenkins that drew him so intensely, he couldn't say, unless it was the need he sensed beneath that brave, tough facade. To have been forced to choose between her husband and her child and then to have lost the child so senselessly was almost more than he could comprehend. Oh, yes, Denise Jenkins was one of the walking wounded with whom he so strongly identified, but those folks were everywhere. And while he empathized, he'd never felt that it was his personal mission to help heal all those other crippled souls. What made Denise different? What created this intense attraction? Was it just that she was beautiful? Belinda, his ex, was beautiful, too, and he'd met any number of highly attractive women since he and Belinda had parted ways. Why now? Why the one woman who wanted nothing to do with him?

He put his hands in his pockets and started walking toward the house, telling himself that Denise's dislike of him was not genuine, that it was fueled by the strength of their attraction, that she was merely frightened. She had been hurt so badly, but why couldn't she see that what she needed to heal that wound completely was a committed, loyal, loving man? What she needed was him. He knew it at the bottom of his soul.

As he stepped up onto the porch and Reiver came to meet him, he reached down automatically and ruffled the dog's ears. Reiver fell into step with him, his nails clicking on the floorboards of the porch at twice the rate of Morgan's own thumping footfalls as they walked toward the door. Both slipped inside, and both in his own way shook off the cold, Reiver plopping down on his rump and yawning so widely that the muscles of his sleek body seemed to roll with it, while Morgan shivered, jaws locked, and rubbed his hands together briskly.

"Bet we have snow by Thanksgiving," he said aloud, wondering if his father could endure another winter on the mountain. He hadn't stretched it too thin when he'd told Denise that he'd welcome her perspective. Yet he couldn't see himself forcing old Ben into a retirement home. He'd welcome his father right here into his own house, but Ben was as set against that as any other plan that caused him to leave behind his beloved mountain cabin, and Morgan's instinctive reaction was to let the old man be. Each and every man bought his own happiness at his own price, provided that he was wise enough to find happiness in the first place, and if Ben's happiness was sustained by that old cabin, well, who was Morgan to tell him that the price was too high? Especially as he knew himself what love of one's home was all about.

He ran a hand lovingly over the flowered paper above the wainscoting and sighed. He'd made this house into a home all by himself. He'd practically rebuilt it board by board over months and months. He'd chosen every stick of furniture and piece of bric-a-brac. It wasn't authentic in the way historians and restorationists demanded. Much of what he had here were reproductions, but each and every item meant something special to him. Every nail had been set with a sense of true accomplishment. Why now did it seem so empty? Why couldn't he stop seeing Denise here, snuggled against him, her bare feet tucked beneath his thigh? Oh, he would warm her so. Heck, he'd set them both on fire. All he needed was a chance, and Sunday at two, his chance would begin.

Chapter Five

Privately Denise had to admit that repeating at least a portion of the drive they had first taken in the dark was an interesting experience. What the view lost in nighttime whimsy, it made up for in perception and color. The hillsides were ablaze with autumn reds and golds, and it struck her suddenly that Thanksgiving was less than six weeks away. She didn't want to think about the holidays. They had been the most difficult times for her since— She shifted in her seat, pushing away thoughts of old losses and unending pain.

"Almost there," Morgan said, misinterpreting her moodiness for restlessness.

She gave him a wan smile and threaded her fingers through her hair. She'd decided to wear it down today, telling herself that she didn't have the energy to put it up. It felt good lying on her shoulders, free from the slightest tug on her scalp. Her old jeans were softly snug against her thighs and calves. The big old sweater that she wore over a sleeveless undershirt was as comfy as a pair of pajamas, even when the stretched-out-vee neckline slid partway off one shoulder. She knew, out of respect for Morgan's father if not Morgan himself, that she ought to have dressed with more care, but she'd felt defiant enough—and depressed enough—not to bother. Morgan, blast him, had swept his gaze over her and said, "Delicious." She hadn't been able to keep still since.

The pickup truck that Morgan used for everyday transportation slowed and made a left turn onto what amounted to little more than a rutted path, despite the rusty mailbox that clung tenaciously to a crooked fence pole beside it. He gunned the gas pedal, propelling the pickup truck up the slope and over some pretty rough gullies and trenches carved in the "road" by water runoff. Denise looked back in concern as Reiver's claws made scrabbling sounds on the bed of the truck.

"Don't worry about him," Morgan said lightly. "He's made this drive hundreds of times. He loves it up here. I don't know how he knows when it's time to come up here, but most Sundays he's waiting in the back of the truck when I get to it, and today was no exception."

"Your father doesn't mind that you bring him along?"

He laughed at that. "Pop will be waiting with a ham bone and a good ear scratching. I'll get my hug second." He shot a look out of the corner of his eye and amended, "Third, most likely, today."

They trundled up into a narrow yard, half of which seemed to be slowly sliding down the face of what had once been a sheer cliff but was now eroded into a tricky fall of loose dirt, clumps of stubborn plants and sharp, scary outcroppings of gray rock. Morgan brought the truck to a halt just feet away from the low porch of a rough cabin cobbled together from logs, stone, planks and tin sheeting. A tendril of wood smoke curled up from the chimney, adding its scent to the pungent aromas of fall leaves, pine mingled with loam and...apple?

The door opened and a stooped gentleman in overalls,

flannel shirt, jean jacket and billed cap stepped out onto the porch. He looked as though he hadn't shaved in a week, his beard a coarse mottle of white, gray and silver with a touch or two of black mixed in. Blue, blue eyes sparkled in the shadow beneath the hat brim.

"Morg," he called out in a voice like the rasp of a file, and then he bent and clapped his hands together at about knee height. "Hey, boy." Reiver bounded out of the back of the truck and nearly knocked the old man off his feet. Morgan's father went down on one knee, laughing and ruffling the dog's fur with hard, rugged hands. Reiver's tail was working at high speed, and he laved the old man's face with his tongue, knocking back his cap. The predicted bone was produced from a coat pocket and snatched with a toothy chomp before being carried to a far corner of the porch and greedily gnawed.

Laughing, the old man pushed himself up, with some effort, to standing again. By that time Morgan had gotten out of the truck and walked around to the passenger side door to help Denise do the same. Morgan led her the few steps to the porch, her hand in his, and said, "Pop, I'd like you to meet Denise Jenkins. Denise, this is my father, Ben."

Ben Holt's eyes, which were a paler version of his son's, flicked over his unexpected guest with obvious interest. "Denise is it?"

"Yes, sir."

His face suddenly split into a wide, denture-white grin. "Welcome, Denise." He stepped down and threw both arms around her, pounding one hand in the center of her back. Almost before she could respond he stepped aside and engulfed Morgan in an even more exuberant embrace. Morgan shot Denise an I-told-you-so smile and wrapped his arms around his father. The affection between them was palpable. After several seconds they pulled apart, and Ben waved a hand to include Denise. "Come on in. I got some cider simmerin' on the stove."

"Ooh." Morgan rubbed his hands together, then slid one of them into the small of her back. "Pop's apple cider is the best around. He used to sell it, but these days he just produces enough for family and friends. You're in for a treat."

"It smells wonderful."

Just then Ben's boots clumped into the doorway. "Well, come on. What ye waitin' fer?"

They hurried up onto the porch and into the house. Denise stopped just inside the door to look around. It was like something out of a movie. The furniture, what there was of it, was roughly hewn and strictly utilitarian. Braided rag rugs covered the rough floor planking. Various animal hides had been tacked up on the walls, along with an impressive set of deer antlers and the hideously ugly, tusked head of a wild boar. A potbellied stove stood across the room from a rock fireplace that looked as though it could come tumbling down at any moment; yet the fire that crackled there seemed especially inviting. At one end of the room, a narrow, open staircase led up through a hole in the ceiling, and beneath it sat a neatly made bed surrounded by pegs in the wall with odds and ends of clothing hanging from them. A single electric light burned overhead, but several old-fashioned glass kerosene lamps sat about the room, one on a small table beside a rocking chair, another next to the bed, and a third in the center of the kitchen stove, a massive wrought-iron affair connected to a propane bottle. Most amazing of all was the water pump that stood proudly on the end of the kitchen counter at the edge of the sink. "Rustic" was an understatement, and though the place was thoroughly ramshackle, it exuded a sense of place and permanence so strong that it literally pulled at her, as if it would draw her in and make her an integral part of the room and the cabin and the mountain itself.

Ben Holt pulled a chair out from the small rectangular table placed just slightly to the left of the center of the room and waved her into it. Then he moved off to bustle around the corner that contained his kitchen, taking out cups and spoons, bowls and small plates and napkins. All the while he talked, the words slow and raspy, as if it had been a long time since he'd spoken aloud.

"You from around these parts, Denise?"

"Originally? No, sir."

"Folks don't stay in one place much no more. Me, I was born right here, and right here is where I aim to die. Morg, now, he ain't wandered too far. But his sister, she's another tale to be told. She might never have lived up on this old mountain, for all the connection she's got to it. And Radley, he's the first generation of Holts to be raised somewheres else, not that he ain't a good boy for all that. A might confused, I s'pose, but a good un. Yer people, now, where from are they?"

"I grew up in Kansas City, Missouri."

"Missouri, eh? I was up in Missouri once back in '48 after the war. Purty country, some of it. Always meant to take Ma up that way for a look-see, but she wasn't much of one for leaving the home place. Won't never leave it now, God rest her, and I'm of the same mind meself. Ever'thing I ever needed to see I could see from this here mountain anyhow." He sighed as he poured steaming cider into the cups. "Lately, all I been seeing on the horizon is Heaven, and I figure I'm closest to it here, so this is where I'm stayin'."

As he said that last, he carried steaming cups to the table and carefully distributed them. Then he sat a small bowl of real butter on the table and spooned a dollop into each cup, ignoring Denise's protest that she really didn't need the extra fat. He chuckled and winked at Morgan. "Never met a man who didn't like a good armful."

Morgan grinned at her over the top of his cup and sipped, closing his eyes to savor the experience. "Ah, Pop, what will I ever do for cider when you're gone?"

Ben smacked his lips appreciatively and shook his head, setting down his own cup. "Some things don't last, son. You and yer sister never had the time to learn the old ways of doing things. My cider, Ma's corn pone, they'll be sweet memories yer life long, just as my own pa's special blend of chew and my ma's mouth harp playin' have stayed sweet for me my whole time. Things that're gone is sometimes the sweetest things of all."

Morgan sipped from his cup and said sadly, "I wonder what sweet things Rad will remember. His mother and I arguing sure won't make for sweet memories." Morgan sighed and stared into his cup as if he might find the answer there. Ben nodded sagely, saying nothing for some time, only to look up at Denise and stagger her with a question she probably should have expected.

"You got children, Denise?"

Her heart dropped like a stone. Suddenly tears blurred her eyes, and she gasped against the sob building in her chest. At once Morgan's hand came across the table and grasped hers. For some reason that gave her the strength and poise to swallow down the lump in her throat and blink back the tears. What was wrong with her? She hadn't reacted so badly in a long time. Shaking her head, she managed a quavering "No." Morgan squeezed her hand, and she stumbled on. "I...I had a son. He died."

Unbearable pain seized her, as fresh as that very day she had first watched Jeremy and his friends set out for the park and then heard them tell her that he was dead. The room shrank to the rim of her cup for several long, torturous seconds. She heard Morgan's whisper but knew instinctively that he was not speaking to her. Gradually a warmth seeped into her, along with a certain presence of mind. She realized then that Morgan was not the only one holding her hand. Ben's gnarled, hoof-tough fingers were curled around one hand, Morgan's strong, firm ones held the other. It was Ben who brought her all the way back, saying in his rough, husky drawl, "I thank God Ma didn't outlive our own younguns, and I pray I won't, either."

It made Denise laugh, not because it was funny, but because she was happy for him and for Morgan's mother, because life had held to its natural rhythm, because they would never know what it meant to lose a life more precious to them than their own. And she prayed—forcefully, silently, wordlessly—that Morgan would never know such loss himself, though he had already had much more time with his son than she had had with hers. That thought brought another, however. She really knew very little about Morgan's son. This seemed the moment to learn.

She cleared her throat and said, "Tell me about Radley. That's your son's name, isn't it, Radley?"

Within moments the mood had shifted a full 180 degrees. Ben got up to pull out a photograph album, while Morgan told her again that Rad was a student at his own alma mater, the University of Arkansas in Fayetteville. Then the stories began, how he'd been terrorized by a curious opossum during one summer sleepover with his grandparents, how he'd used that experience to frighten the pants off the friends whom he frequently brought up the mountain with him. On a certain hunting trip those same friends had turned the tables on him by secretly capturing an opossum and zipping the poor thing into Radley's sleeping bag in the middle of the night. The stories went on. Ben spoke proudly of how eleven-year-old Rad had shot the boar, whose head decorated his wall, after it had chased Ben himself up a tree. They laughed about fish that got away and baseballs that didn't, about first dates and proms. In the end Morgan spoke of the way the breakup of his marriage had affected his only child, of his own regrets and the confidence he felt about the rightness of the ultimate decisions Radley still had to make about his life. Dusk had settled over the mountain before the subject was in any way exhausted.

"We're going to have to think about going," Morgan said regretfully.

"Here now, who's gonna read me my chapters?" Ben protested, and he got up to fetch a worn, yellowed Bible with a number of the pages now lying loose between the cracked leather covers. With it, he placed a kerosene lamp on the table. Morgan lit the lamp and adjusted the wick, explaining that Ben had read a chapter from each of the Old and the New Testament of the Bible every Sunday for over forty years. Now that his eyes had gotten too bad for him to read the words for himself, Morgan read them aloud to him. As he began on the New Testament chapter, Ben refilled their cups with steaming cider and settled down to listen. The thirteenth chapter of Romans was not a long one, but the third chapter of Numbers contained fifty-one verses listing the families of the Levites and instructions to Moses concerning setting them aside for the priesthood. Halfway through the Numbers reading, Ben interrupted and suggested that Denise finish up while Morgan went out to the smokehouse before it got any darker out and brought in a couple pieces of meat for the week ahead.

"Do you mind?" Morgan asked her, sliding the book toward her side of the table. She shook her head and picked up the Bible. Morgan clapped a hand on his father's shoulder as he moved toward the door, and Ben told him in detail which pieces of meat he wanted brought inside.

After Morgan went out to do as he was requested and Denise had begun reading the verses from the Bible, Ben laid a hand on her wrist to silence her. "I wanted a moment alone with you," he admitted gruffly. "I want you to know, I'll be restin' easier tonight for havin' met you. My

Morg ain't never brought no woman up here before, not since his divorce, so I know yer somethin' special to him, and I want you to know, too, that he's a good son, a'ways was. He'll comfort you, if you let 'im. Seemed fer a while that he sorta forgot what was important, but them times're gone, an' now all he needs is someone to love, someone to comfort him in his hurtin', cause hurtin' comes t' all of us, and there's no help for it, no help at all. Morg, he knows how to love, he surely does, and I don't mind tellin' it. Fact is, I'm proud of 'im, and I'm purely pleased, I am, about the two of you.''

Morgan's footsteps clumped on the porch then, but instead of coming in he called the dog until, far in the distance, Denise could hear Reiver barking. Only then did Morgan come inside to lay two brownish, wrinkled pieces of meat on the table.

''Are these the ones you wanted, Pop?''

'''Zactly the two,'' Ben declared, smiling up at Morgan.

''Reiver's on his way in,'' Morgan said, looking at Denise. ''We'd best be loading up.''

Denise got up and started to carry her cup to the counter, but Ben stopped her with his own hands. ''Naw, comp'ny don't wash up. Besides, I got me nothin' better to do on a Sunday evenin'.''

Leaving the cup on the table, Denise smiled at the old man. ''Thank you, Ben, for the cider and the welcome.''

He patted her shoulders and scratched her cheek with a dry kiss. ''You come on back now, hear?''

''I—I'll try,'' Denise whispered uncertainly. ''You take care.''

''Honey, all the care's already been taken. There ain't nothin' left for me now but Heaven, an' I'm sure ready.'' He said it joyfully, shaming her for the grief she felt at the thought of his dying. He hugged and kissed Morgan then, saying, ''I love ye, son.''

"I love you, too, Pop. When I come next week I'll shave you."

Ben chuckled and explained to Denise that he couldn't see well enough to shave his own face in the mirror anymore, so how he looked no longer bothered him. "But Ma," he said, "she liked to keep up appearances, so occasionally I get scraped, just in case we meet up at the pearly gates." He scratched his chin, saying, "I swear if I showed up there like this she'd just send me back, halo and all, fer a razor." He laughed when he said it, and Denise marveled at the humor and joy and utter normalcy he found in the prospect of his own death.

They took their leave, Reiver prancing around them with eager pants on their way to the truck. Ben gave the dog another hug and a pat and ordered him into the back of the truck. Then he stood in the warm glow of the light that spilled from the open doorway and waved until he disappeared in the rearview mirror. Denise found herself weeping again, but oddly, she wasn't sad. She was touched. She was...grateful.

And she was afraid.

She was afraid that she'd found something very special in Morgan Holt, something too special to hold at bay. And it was going to turn her carefully constructed life upside down. *Hurtin' comes t' all of us, and there's no help for it.*

No help at all.

They drove in silence for some time. When it felt right, Morgan spoke. "So what do you think?"

She took a deep breath as if awakening from a deep slumber and said, "About?"

"My father."

"He's wonderful."

"Yes, he is, but you can see why my sister is worried."

She said nothing for some minutes and then, ''Can nothing be done about his eyes?''

''No. Some years ago perhaps, but not now.''

''I'm sorry.''

''That is the most obvious problem, I suppose, but the greatest problem is his heart. The doctors say he's been living on borrowed time for years.''

She sighed and lifted a hand to her hair, her elbow braced against the window. ''I think he's been living for you,'' she said softly. ''He wants you to be happy. He wants you not to be alone.''

He knew it was true and that it wouldn't help to say that he wanted the same thing. He said, ''So what do you think about him living on alone there?''

''He doesn't even have a telephone,'' she pointed out.

''No, but the neighbors come by and check on him every day.''

''It isn't safe,'' she argued, ''all those propane bottles and kerosene lamps.''

''No, it isn't safe,'' he agreed.

''He doesn't even have indoor plumbing.''

''No plumbing.''

She stared straight ahead through the windshield, and after a few moments she lifted a hand to wipe her fingertips across her cheeks. ''Leaving there would kill him.''

''Yes, very likely it would.''

Silence came again, tentative, sad, unsettled. They had almost reached the Fayetteville bypass when she turned to look at him and said, ''You won't let your sister move him, will you?''

He met her gaze levelly. ''No. I won't let anyone move him.''

She wiped her cheeks again, sniffed and said, ''I haven't cried this much in years.''

He reached across the seat and took her hand in his. ''Some tears are healing,'' he told her gently. She turned her face away, but she let him hold her hand. He drove them slowly but surely around Fayetteville and headed southeast.

They were almost home when she said abruptly, "Some wounds can't be healed."

He thought his reply through carefully. "I believe they can. The scars remain, and sometimes they cripple us, but the wounds don't have to remain raw."

She said nothing more. He pulled the truck up into the drive beside the house. She pulled her hand free of his and reached for the door handle. "Thank you," he said quickly, then added as nonchalantly as he could, "Will I see you tomorrow?"

He could feel her panic, her trepidation, and decided that he would tell her that she was free to do as she pleased. But he couldn't. He couldn't make the words come out, couldn't throw away his one chance. Instead he said, "Pop was right, you know. I'm good at loving."

"You were listening," she accused tiredly.

"Yes."

"You knew what he wanted to say to me."

"Yes."

She opened the door and slid a foot out of it, but then she turned back, her face a mask of pure sorrow. "I can't love you, Morgan. I can't."

He wanted to put his hands on her, to pull her back inside with him, to hold her, but he didn't dare. He had to settle for draping an arm over the steering wheel and turning partway in his seat to communicate his urgency. "Listen to me for a moment, please. My parents taught me how to love. They were good teachers."

"I can see that."

"But somehow I forgot for a time," he went on quickly, "and when I remembered again I found I had no one to love, not the way I want to love, not the way I need to love."

"It's not me, Morgan!" she cried. "Why can't you see that?"

He shook his head and said, "I don't know. I just can't. I just can't."

She made a strangled sound, something between anger and pain, and then she bolted. She pushed the door wide and she ran.

He laid his head against the steering wheel and tried to catch his breath. He closed his eyes, but all he could see was Denise at the table with his father and him, smiling, relaxed, her hair tumbling over her shoulders, free—if only for the moment—of her own heartsickness.

Reiver jumped down out of the back of the truck and stuck his head into the open door of the cab as if to ask what was holding things up. "Coming, boy," he said apologetically. "Just the two of us for dinner again, I guess. Just me and you. Just…me."

But it couldn't always be that way. He wouldn't let himself believe that it would always be that way, not for him—and not for Denise Jenkins.

Denise fumbled with the key, turning it first one direction and then another until finally the door pulled free. She rushed inside, yanked it shut and threw the dead bolt before she even turned on the light. The neat, efficient, modern comfort literally assaulted her. The central heating kicked on, but she shivered uncontrollably, cold from the inside out. Her head was full of flashing images. Ben Holt rubbing that monster of a dog, carrying hot cider to the table, laughing about Radley, kissing her cheek, holding her hand. She saw Ben. She felt Morgan.

Standing close, strong, quiet, patient, he waited to dry her tears, to hold her together, to make her smile. He wanted to love her, to make her happy, to stop the pain. She knew with awful certainty that she could never let him do that. She knew, finally, that she did not want to stop the pain. She cherished her pain. Without her pain she had nothing left of Jeremy, nothing left of the son for whom she'd gladly have given up her own life.

How could she be happy when her son was dead? How could she live, really live, when he did not? She couldn't. She didn't even want to, and it was selfish of Morgan to even ask it of her. He had so much already. He had peace and contentment and freedom. She had only memories and the pain of a love that she could not, would not, give up. Jeremy was dead. She wouldn't allow her love for him to die, too, no matter that it meant keeping the pain alive, as well. No, Morgan was asking too much. He had to see that he was asking too much.

She wanted to think that Ben would understand the depth of her loss, but she couldn't let that matter. She couldn't let anything matter more than the loss of her son. She had her job. That was enough to fill her days and even her nights. That was all she wanted, all she needed. Except Jeremy. Except her son. He was the one person she could never again have to hold. Nothing and no one could replace him, not even Morgan Holt.

She felt a prick on her foot above the top of her shoe and looked down to find Smithson delicately sinking his hind claws into her sock as he regally, deliberately walked across it. She bent down and scooped him up. "Ready for some attention, are you?" He craned his upper body away from her, but she wasn't fooled. She carried him to the chair in front of the window and sat down to devote some time to serious stroking and crooning. Smithson promptly settled down in her lap and allowed her to minister to him without so much as a cuddle. She didn't mind. She liked her space, too, and she understood all about putting some-one in her—or his—place. They understood each other, she and Smithson. Together they had everything they really needed.

Morgan Holt was just going to have to accept that.

Sometimes life didn't give a person any choice, and the situation with his father was a case in point. It was a problem without a solution, and if Morgan could accept that, he could accept the fact that the two of them had no future together. She hated to hurt him. He was a good man. She saw that very clearly now. But facts were facts, and no one could change them. No one.

Feeling fortified again, calmer, stronger, she put down the cat and climbed the stairs to the bedroom, flipping on lights as she went. The message light on the answering machine was blinking from the bedside table. She walked over and pushed it, listening to the techno squawk and then the sound of her brother's voice.

"Hey, sis! Hope you're not working. Listen, May and the kids and I are driving down to Texas to see her parents next weekend. We thought we'd swing by on Saturday for a little visit with you. Haven't seen you in several months. Mom says you're not sure you can get home for the holidays. I'd like to change your mind about that. The folks won't be around forever, you know. Anyway, we'll be through Jasper about ten Saturday morning and we'll see you then. May says not to worry about lun—"

The techno squawk cut him off. Her hard-won composure vanished. She plopped down on the side of her bed and pulled at her hair, gritting her teeth to keep from screaming. That was all she needed, Troy and May and their two kids, the perfect little family. She didn't want to see them. She didn't want to dredge up the love that she knew was buried deep in her heart for these people. She didn't want to work at being pleasant and pretending that she didn't care that she no longer had a family of her own. She didn't want to see the worry in her brother's eyes or the pity in May's—or the unease in Cory's and Missy's small faces.

She understood how they felt. If it could happen to Jeremy, it could happen to them, too. If she was their mother, she'd be worried sick every moment they were out of her sight. Even now she worried for them, but the fact remained that she didn't want to see them. She had to derail this impending visit, and she vowed that no matter what, Troy wouldn't talk her into going home for the holidays. She wouldn't do that to herself. Or to them.

She picked up the telephone and punched in the eleven appropriate numbers. May answered, realized who was calling and switched to a too-bright voice before going to get Troy. He came on sounding a little defensive and a lot wary.

"Denise?"

"Hello, little brother."

"Everything okay?"

"Sure. I'm just really busy, that's all. You know how it is."

"Yeah, me, too. That's the reason I decided to take this time off. The kids have a couple of days out of school next week, and we won't have another chance to get down that way again until after Christmas. If you're serious about not coming home for the holidays, this may be our only chance to see you all year."

"Uh, yeah, listen, about the holidays, I...I have obligations here."

"Oh? You seeing someone?"

"That's not the point, Troy."

"You can't spend the holidays there alone moping."

"I can do anything I please, thank you."

He sighed, and she could feel his frustration and concern. I'm worried about you, Deni," he said softly. "I need to know you're okay."

"I'm fine. I just—"

"Can't you spare a couple of hours for us, sis? Are you going to cut us completely out of your life, us and everyone else?"

"Of course not. I just—"

"Then we'll see you Saturday."

"Troy..." She bit her lip. What could she say that wouldn't wound him? What excuse would he not see through? She put her fingertips to one temple and capitulated. "Tell May I'll put together something for lunch."

His relief rang through every word. "Oh, that's not necessary. We'll go out."

"No. No, I want to."

"Okay, sure, but don't go to any real trouble."

Real trouble. God love him, he didn't know what real trouble was. She spared a wish that he never would and said something inane about her silly cat enjoying company, then rang off to flop back on the bed and groan. Why couldn't anyone understand? Her son was dead. Her life could never, ever be normal or happy again. It hurt her just to see a whole family together, but seeing her brother's family was even worse. They'd always expected to raise their children together as they had been raised, surrounded by cousins and siblings. That could never happen now, not for her. All she had left was her grief, and she wouldn't give that up even if it meant that she could no longer unselfishly love her brother's family. Even if it meant always being alone.

She struggled up into a sitting position, telling herself that she could manage a weekend visit. It was the lifetime of togetherness that was truly beyond her. She pretended to function normally all the time. She could pretend a little harder come Saturday. She only hoped that would be enough for Troy, because anything more was beyond her just now. She looked down as Smithson wound himself sensuously around her ankles.

"You're the only one who doesn't expect me to get over it," she told him, scratching him delicately between the ears. "You and Ben. You're the only ones who can understand."

Chapter Six

"It's a lovely little apartment," May said, beaming a too-bright smile as she dropped down onto the sofa. She groped for her husband's hand, obviously in need of support, and Troy was nothing if not supportive. He squeezed her fingers and looked up at Denise, doing his part to keep the nonconversation flowing.

"Yeah, it's, uh, kind of an unusual setup, though, a modern apartment building and a restored Victorian manor on the same lot, more or less."

"Well, that's because they're owned by the same man," Denise informed him lightly. "And Jasper's not a big city, you know. They don't seem to have the same kind of restrictions and zoning as, well, Fayetteville, for example."

"That's sort of my point," Troy said, leaning forward and taking May's hand with him. His sleek, dark head craned back so that he could stare up at Denise from beneath the smooth line of his brow. "Seems like an attractive, single, young woman like yourself would want to be more in the center of things. How come you moved here instead of Fayetteville? And don't say it's because the office is practically next door, because Fayetteville isn't that far away.''

Exasperated, she said, ''The road runs both ways, you know.''

From overhead came the sound of a loud thump, drawing all eyes upward. May and Troy looked at each other in sudden wariness. ''Where are the kids?''

''I thought they were right behind you when we came back downstairs.''

May jumped up. ''I'd better go and get them.''

Smithson apparently agreed, if his yowl from the same general area was any indication. Concerned for both cat and children, Denise muttered that she'd go with May, and set off behind her.

This visit was going just as she'd feared it would. Troy and May were as uncomfortable as she. Conversation so far had been rife with pregnant pauses and touchy subjects. The children were tired of being indoors, and she knew that she had been impatient with them. The tour of the apartment had taken too little time and succeeded only in interesting the children in her surly cat. And Troy kept returning to the subject of her ''emotional isolation.'' She had the feeling that they weren't done with it, yet.

To add to her already overflowing cup, she was halfway up the stairs when someone knocked at the door. She stopped and yelled, ''Coming!'' But Smithson yowled again just then and started hissing. She spared no moment to consider who might be calling or why. Instead, she hung over the banister and yelled for Troy to answer the door, then sprinted up the remaining steps. Let him deal with whoever had the poor timing to show up just then. She had all she could handle just now between her darn cat, two precocious kids and a brother with too much concern. She just had too much of everything right now. Too much of nothing.

* * *

Morgan stared at the tall, dark man standing in Denise's doorway and felt his heart drop to the soles of his feet. He saw a certain familiarity in the straight, even features and tall, slender body shape but could not for the moment think beyond finding a handsome stranger at Denise's door. His tone was—understandably, he felt—sharp when he demanded, "Who are you?"

The stranger cocked his head, as if searching for and finding a certain hoped-for note in Morgan's voice. "I'm Troy. Who are you?"

"Morgan. Is Denise home?"

A smile grew on the stranger's face. "Yeah. She's upstairs rescuing the cat. Want to come in?"

Morgan nodded and stepped up into the tiny foyer, pulling the door closed behind him. "Something wrong with Smithson?"

Troy's smile grew even broader. "You know Denise's cat?"

Morgan wondered if this conversation was as weird as he thought it was. He shrugged. "I'm pretty much a dog person myself, but yeah, I know about Denise's cat. What I don't know about is you."

"Oh!" The other man stuck out his hand. "I thought I said. It's Troy, Troy Jenkins."

"Jenkins!" Morgan put his hand in Troy's only a tad belatedly. "You're kin to Denise in some way then?"

"I'm her brother. She took her maiden name back after the divorce," he explained.

Her brother! "Oh, yeah," Morgan said, pumping the other man's hand enthusiastically now that he knew he wasn't looking at the competition. "From Missouri, right?"

"Springfield."

"Hey, it's great to meet you. I had no idea you were coming to visit."

Troy finally took his hand back, saying, "We're just stopping over for an hour or two."

"We?"

"May and the kids and I. May, that's my wife, her parents live in Texas, and the kids have a couple days out of school at the beginning of the week, so we thought, Why not drive down for a visit and stop by Denise's on the way?"

"Right. I see. Well, it's nice to meet you."

"You, too." Troy ducked his head and rubbed the toe of one shoe against the carpet, adding, "How, um, how long have you two known each other? You and my sister, I mean."

"Oh, since before she even moved in," Morgan said, deliberately painting himself once more in his assigned role as boyfriend. This was getting to be a real habit, one that he had no inclination to break. Painted often enough, the portrait was bound to be taken for reality at some point, even by Denise.

Troy literally beamed. "Really? That's great!"

"What's great?" Denise said, rounding the foot of the stairs and coming across the foyer, Smithson in her arms. She stopped where she was when she saw Morgan. "What are you doing here?"

He didn't know what to say other than the truth, though he'd expected a more private moment to press his advantage. "I, ah, just wanted to make sure we're still on for tomorrow."

"Tomorrow?"

"It's Sunday. Pop will be expecting us," he said pointedly.

Color immediately suffused Denise's face, anger sparking in her dark eyes. She opened her mouth, no doubt to denounce his heavy-handedness, then glanced at her brother and abruptly snapped her mouth shut again.

Troy, who seemed completely unaware of the awkward-

ness, beamed on the whole room and happily announced,
"That's great! Sounds like...one big happy family!" He
grinned at Denise. "Where's May? I want her to meet
Morgan. And the kids, too. Oh. Is everything okay up
there?"

Denise nodded wanly. "Yes, fine," but as Troy moved
to the foot of the stairs to call down his wife and children,
she glared at Morgan, who surreptitiously shrugged his
shoulders as if to say that he didn't know what was eating
her. Actually, he had a pretty good idea what was going
on here. Like any normal, loving brother, Troy was worried
about his sister being alone, and he assumed—perhaps he
even sensed—that Morgan was more than just her landlord.
Come to think of it, Troy probably didn't even know that
he was her landlord; so as far as he was concerned, Morgan
had only one reason for being in Denise's life. Morgan
didn't have to think too hard before deciding that it would
be in his best interest not to enlighten anyone.

A small, attractive woman with shoulder-length caramel
blond hair came down the stairs flanked by two children,
a boy and a girl of elementary-school age. Both had the
same dark, sleek hair as their father and aunt. Troy herded
them all into the living room, making introductions as they
went. "This is May, my better half, and Cory—he's nine.
And Missy is six. May, this is Morgan— Uh, I'm sorry..."

Morgan stepped forward to take May Jenkins's small
hand in his. "Holt. Morgan Holt."

She smiled uncertainly and looked to her husband for
further explanation. Troy slipped his hands into his pants
pockets and rocked back onto his heels, still grinning like
an idiot. "Morgan is Denise's, ah..."

"Friend," Morgan supplied easily, well aware that his
tone implied much more than mere friendship, but then,
why shouldn't it?

May gasped and her grip tightened. "That's wonderful!'' She abruptly switched her gaze to Denise. ''Why didn't you tell us?''

Morgan released her hand and pretended to scratch his nose, head bowed to hide a grimace. This was the moment Denise would either choose to go along or denounce him as insane. She glared and sputtered and finally came out with, ''W-well, it's p-personal!''

Morgan's grimace transformed into a smile, but he figured he'd pressed his luck as far as was advisable. Stepping close to Denise, he said conversationally, ''I don't want to intrude.'' He smiled at Denise, ignoring her very pointed glare. ''I just wanted to remind you about tomorrow. Same time as usual?''

She lifted a brow to let him know that he was going to pay for this later. ''Two?''

He smiled to let her know that he was willing to pay whatever price she exacted. ''Right. Two o'clock. Well, I'll see you then.'' He nodded at everyone in general, then bowed his head and pressed a quick kiss to Denise's temple, intending to make his escape before her temper blew.

But Troy and May were too delighted at the fact of his involvement in Denise's life to let him go that easily. ''No, stay for lunch,'' Troy insisted, poking him playfully on the shoulder. ''We're just getting to know each other.''

May added her support. ''Denise has made a mountain of sandwiches, and we can always open another can of soup.''

Smithson even joined in, suddenly leaping from Denise's arms onto Morgan's shoulder. The kids laughed and started trying to call the cat to them, while Smithson ignored them and batted at the light fixture hanging over Morgan's head. Everyone laughed at that, even Denise, though the deeper expression in her eyes was one of irritation. Disappointment welled up inside him. She didn't want him around even now. Looking down into her face, he said softly, ''I'd better go.''

The look in her eyes softened, warmed. "Stay if you want," she said, somewhat less than graciously. As if that settled it, she switched her attention to the cat. "Come down from there, you opportunist, and leave that alone."

Smithson meowed as she plucked him off Morgan's shoulder and dropped him on the floor. Quick as lightning, he streaked up the stairs. Missy darted after him, but her mother caught her about the shoulders and pulled her back. "Oh, no, you don't. You've tormented that poor cat enough."

Missy crumpled her face and started to cry, despite a terse scolding from her father. Sensing that he could serve Denise and her family as well as himself, Morgan went down on one knee and took both her little hands in his. "Hey, you like dogs?"

Missy's face smoothed, and she nodded her head vigorously.

"That's great! You know why? Because my dog Reiver loves to play."

"Morgan, that's like playing with an elephant!" Denise objected.

"Aw, they'll get along fine," he assured her. "Reiver's great with kids." In an aside to Missy he said from the corner of his mouth. "It's cats that he hates. But don't worry," he added to Denise, "I won't leave them alone."

"Reiver and Missy or Reiver and Smithson?" Troy joked.

"Both!"

"Can I, Mom?" Missy begged, jumping up and down.

May looked at Morgan, then at her husband and finally at Denise. "Oh, all right, but just until Aunt Denise and I get lunch ready."

"Me, too!" Cory said, and Troy laid a hand on top of the boy's head.

"We'll all go meet this dog who loves to play."

"There's plenty to go around," Morgan joked, hopping

to his feet and heading toward the door. He shot a look at
Denise as the Jenkins kids grabbed coats and caps.

"Twenty minutes," she said sternly. "Tops."

"Yes, ma'am."

Troy pushed open the door, and they all tumbled out
onto the walk. "At least the sun's out," he heard May
saying as he closed the door behind them.

He glanced upward into the clear blue sky and grinned.
The day was brighter than May knew. "Reiver! Here,
boy!"

The dog bounded off the porch and came to a sliding
stop at Morgan's feet. Intimidated by the sheer size of him,
the kids clapped their hands but stayed back. Laughing,
Morgan got down on all fours and made an idiot of himself. Saying, "Watch this," to the kids, he proceeded to
pretend to be a dog himself, panting and barking, wagging
his imaginary tail, whining and rolling onto his back, legs
squirming. This was an old game, and Reiver matched his
master's antics to the letter, even to the tones of his bark
and whine. But when Morgan got up to brush himself off,
Reiver stayed on his back, begging for a tummy rub. At
Morgan's nod, the kids fell on the dog, giggling and laughing as they tried to rub Reiver without getting licked to
within an inch of their lives.

Morgan got Troy into the game by snatching off Missy's
cap and tossing it to him. Reiver instantly came up and
went after it. A spirited game of keep-away ensued, during
which Reiver got the cap and teased Missy with it, giving
her a chance to catch up before darting away. Morgan assured Troy that the cap wouldn't be damaged, and Troy
seemed to accept that without question. Meanwhile, much
to the kids' delight, Reiver played a spirited game, even
jumping over Missy's head at one point. Another time the
wily dog dropped the cap on the ground, panting as if to
say he'd had it, only to snatch it up again and bolt away
when Cory made a grab for it. Finally, Morgan called the

dog to him and ordered the cap's release. Reiver complied, happily dropping it and his large body at Morgan's feet to pant and lick anyone who came within tongue's reach. Morgan briefly examined the cap, then passed it to Troy, who subjected it to a much more thorough examination. Shaking his head to indicate his amazement, he plunked the cap onto Missy's head. Missy was too busy hugging Reiver to notice.

The inevitable questions came then. What kind? How old? How was he trained? Can we get one, Dad? Ple-e-ease. Morgan was both proud and regretful to inform them that Reiver was one of a kind. He talked to the kids about the time and patience involved in bringing a dog up to such a level of camaraderie. Cory was particularly avid for details, and Morgan explained as carefully as he could what was involved in finding, training and caring for such an animal. Afterward, Cory very manfully asked his father to consider letting him get a dog for Christmas, going so far as to promise to give up an expensive computer game that he'd previously requested. A surprised Troy promised that they'd discuss the matter further with May at another time. It was Morgan who suggested smilingly that being on their best behavior wouldn't hurt their case when they discussed the decision with their mother. From that moment on, they were the two best behaved, mannerly youngsters he'd ever met.

Lunch came off much easier than Morgan had expected. The conversation was animated, the food simple but wholesome. Troy and May included him in everything without the slightest sign of awkwardness. Much time was given to describing the dog and his antics, but Morgan changed the subject when he realized that Denise seemed disturbed by it. If she never spoke directly to or about him, he supposed that was only to be expected and hoped the Jenkinses didn't notice. They did not appear to. When May began clearing the table, saying that it was time they got

on the road again, Morgan quickly excused himself in order to give the family time to say their goodbyes and spare
himself the dressing-down he knew he deserved. After
thanking Denise for the lunch, he shook hands once again
with Troy and, to his surprise, got hugs from the kids. Cory
even asked if it would be possible for Morgan to help with
the dog he hoped to talk his mother into getting for him.
Troy rescued Morgan from an awkward reply by saying
that he was sure they'd be seeing one another again before
long, and that was that. All in all, it had been a very pro-
ductive day, to Morgan's mind, at least.

Denise was not sure whether to be grateful or resentful
of Morgan Holt's inclusion in her brother's visit. His appearance had forestalled further comment and perhaps even
an argument concerning what Troy saw as her "emotional
isolation," but Denise could not help thinking that another
visit with Morgan to his father's home was a high—and
dangerous—price to pay for what could be at best a temporary reprieve. On the other hand, Troy and May were
happier believing that Denise had a man in her life again,
and Denise was not foolish enough to worry them unnec-
essarily.

Nevertheless, she'd felt more than a twinge of guilt
when Troy had taken her aside to say how very much he
liked Morgan, and she could not quite fully suppress the
thrill she'd felt when Troy had jokingly divulged that Morgan had seemed more than a little jealous before he'd realized that he was speaking to her brother. She was even
disturbed—she hesitated to say envious—that Morgan's
great, hulking dog had been such a hit with the children
when Smithson had done nothing but hiss and yowl and
prove himself thoroughly unapproachable. Because her pet
was unapproachable that didn't mean that she was unapproachable, did it? Keeping her mouth shut and letting

Troy think what he liked wasn't the same as admitting that he was right to call her emotionally isolated. Was it?

She pushed away such thoughts, but she didn't cavil at keeping her appointment with Morgan for the next day. She was glad, afterward, that she hadn't. Ben welcomed her with the same easy acceptance as before, but that day they did not go inside immediately and sit at the table. Instead, they went for a stroll, Ben pointing out features of interest with the knobby cane he used to support himself. He told amusing stories of Morgan's childhood and talked with aching longing of his wife and parents. And yet, he was a happy man, content with his lot in life, attached spiritually and emotionally to the place of his birth and that of his children. Denise sensed no self-pity in him, and it was obvious that he loved wisely, deeply and with an uncommonly pragmatic maturity. Would not such a man produce just such a son?

But that was another thought she did not want to think, and it was laughably easy to put such troubling notions aside there on the mountaintop. This place offered peace, and she fully understood Morgan's quiet assertion that he would never change a thing about it, that it would always serve to "center" him. She knew that in saying this he was making an unspoken promise to his father, and Ben knew it as well. Such closeness between the two men produced a melancholy in Denise that she did not fully understand. Yet she knew that at one time she had shared a measure of such closeness with members of her own family. Oddly, though, neither the reluctantly accepted knowledge nor the melancholy it produced truly disturbed the otherworldly peace that she found here.

Her mind became a comfortable blank. The silence that fell over the cab of the truck as she and Morgan made the journey home felt appropriate and safe. So she was as surprised as Morgan when she heard herself blurting out a very personal question.

"Do you ever wish you had more children?" It was something she'd wondered before. In fact, the question of children and whether or not to have more had kept her from developing an interest in a second marriage. To her, having another child would be merely an attempt to replace Jeremy, and nothing and no one could ever do that. It wouldn't be fair for her to have another child. It wouldn't be fair for her to make a commitment to a man who wanted children with her.

Morgan sent her a clearly bemused look, then set himself to thinking over his answer. "No, not really. I wouldn't have minded more, but Radley's everything I could hope for, and I certainly wouldn't want to start fresh now. Why do you ask?"

She shrugged to buy herself time to come up with a safe answer, finally saying, "I don't know. You seemed to get on so well with my brother's kids."

"I like kids," he said. "That doesn't mean I feel an overwhelming need to father them all."

"I used to like kids," she said quietly.

"Until you lost your own," he supplied gently. "I can understand that. It must be an especially excruciating kind of torture to see your brother's happy, healthy children running around making havoc that Jeremy will never make again."

Suddenly Denise was sobbing, doubled over with the pain of a loss so great that it truly felt unbearable. She didn't realize that Morgan had pulled the truck off the narrow road until she felt his arms come around her.

"I'm sorry, honey. I'm so sorry. I only wanted to let you know that I understand."

She shook her head. "You used his name," she said. "No one ever uses his name anymore. It's like he never was. He's gone, so they forget him. But I can't! I won't!"

"And you shouldn't," Morgan told her, rocking her gently. "You should treasure every delightful memory, every instant of his life. Don't forget a moment of it, not the good, not the bad.''

Denise felt as if someone had hit her between the eyes with a hammer. The good, the delightful. Dear God, when was the last time she remembered anything but the pain? One thought of Jeremy and she saw his coffin, heard the doctor saying that he was gone, blood spattered on the pavement, squealing tires, his crumpled little body, vacant eyes. What had happened to the times when he had patted her cheeks, first with tiny hands and then with surprisingly strong and capable ones, and said that he loved her? What had happened to the indecipherable drawings for the bestest mommy in the world, the giggling fits, the Halloween costumes, the Christmas mornings? How could she forget tiny die-cast cars and superhero comics and tape-recorded animal sounds and bubbles floating on the afternoon air? Shouldn't she remember birthday parties and the circus and baths and bedtime stories?

She closed her eyes and memories flooded her. She gasped, remembering the day Jeremy's grandfather had proudly presented him a handmade slingshot, the window that was almost immediately broken, Jeremy sitting in the corner in his grandfather's lap, while she and her mother tried not to laugh at the pair of them as they waited out their punishment. When was the last time she'd told her own father that she loved him or giggled when her mother rolled her eyes at something silly he'd said? They must miss, just as she did, the feel of Jeremy's arms wound tightly around their necks, the weight of his little body as he slept on their laps. She heard herself saying, ''He loved bubble gum.''

Morgan chuckled. ''So did Rad. Man, he used to blow bubbles the size of his head, and then they'd burst and I'd have to peel it off his face, out of his eyebrows, even.''

Oh, could she relate to that! ''Jeremy kept falling asleep with it in his mouth, and I'd either forget to check for it or I'd run my finger around his mouth and not find it, and then he'd wake up the next morning with it in his hair.'' She shook her head, smiling despite the tears.

"How'd you get it out?" he wanted to know, loosening his hold a bit.

"I've tried everything, peanut butter, ice, machine oil, sand. Nothing really works but cutting it out. We practically had to shave his head once. I thought, 'Now he'll remember to spit it out!' Then when I had it down to a kind of fringe around the hairline, he said, 'Leave it there, Mom! Leave it there!' He just insisted. He thought it was so cool! So I sent him outside to play, thinking the other kids were going to laugh and jeer at him and that, finally, would teach him a lesson." She shook her head. The laughter crept up on her, spilling out when she least expected it.

Morgan squeezed her. "Go on. What happened?"

She still marvelled at it. "Two, three days later, I notice all the kids in the neighborhood are going around sporting these really short haircuts with this long, ugly fringe around the hairline. One of the boys' mothers actually said to me, 'We just can't get it to look like Jeremy's. What hairstylist do you take him to?'"

Morgan chortled, his arms looped easily about her, one hand spread possessively over her ribs. "Sounds like he was a trendsetter, one of those totally confident kids so secure, so loved, that even if the other kids had teased him it wouldn't have fazed him in the least."

"I guess so," she said, lost in her memories.

"Sounds like you were a very good mother," Morgan told her softly. "Sounds like you were able to make up for his father's lack of involvement."

"Do you think so?" she asked, praying that he was right.

"Absolutely. You must have been remarkably devoted. Jeremy sounds like a very happy boy."

"They said he didn't feel any pain," she whispered, speaking of his death. "They said he never knew what happened, he couldn't have had time to be afraid."

"He wouldn't have," Morgan said. "The body is designed so that shock delays both emotional and physical pain. He would have been gone before he could feel any of that."

"I know what you mean," she said. "I couldn't believe it when they first told me, because I couldn't feel it yet."

"Yes."

"But I've felt it every day since."

"Yes," he said again, conveying in that one word a world of understanding. And then, very deliberately, he kissed her. His hand settled on her throat and gently slid upward to push her head back and cup her chin, tilting her face to his so that his mouth could settle, oh, so lightly, over hers. For a few sweet seconds he kept the pressure light, his lips clinging tenderly to hers. She didn't try to stop him, didn't want to stop him, and he must have sensed that, for he gently pulled his mouth from hers, cleared his throat, released her safety belt, and proceeded to turn her upside down and inside out. Before she even knew what was happening to her, he had her on his lap, his hands under her sweater, and his tongue down her throat. And still she couldn't do anything but hang on and let it rip.

Rip it did, right along every nerve ending, burning and soothing in the same flash and leaving a desperate awareness in its path. She had not consciously, willingly felt so much in years, and she realized with mingled dismay and relief that she needed it, craved it. Him. What she needed, what she wanted, was him. But how…why…what if…? All the questions and doubts were right there, ready to ambush her…and she made the decision to push them away, to be normal again, even if it meant being needy and desperate and foolish.

She wrapped her arms around his neck and fought back

with every feminine wile she possessed—and had him panting and trembling within seconds. For the first time in a long time, she truly felt that she was in control, and she knew suddenly that control was what she'd been working so hard to achieve. Funny how she may have found it just by letting go. But she was in no mood to analyze. She was in the mood to feel, and what she wanted to feel was Morgan.

With only that thought in mind, she straddled him, negotiating her position clumsily in the confined space until she could rest on her knees, her legs spread wide to span his thighs. He released his hold on her, but refused to relinquish her mouth, cupping her face with his hands to prevent her from pulling away, not that she wanted to. She wanted just the opposite, in fact, and when she pushed his jacket off his shoulders and began forcing the sleeves down his arms, he finally seemed to understand and broke the kiss just long enough to get out of it and yank his T-shirt off over his head.

When he pulled her head back down to his, she laughed and let her hands roam over the solid muscles of his chest and arms, marveling at the crispness of reddish brown hair and the warmth of his skin. He made a sound deep in his throat, and his arms came around her again, pulling her tight against him. She slid her hands over his shoulders and pushed them down between his back and the back of the seat, all the way down to the waistband of his jeans and downward still to the tautness of his buttocks. Groaning, he slid to the edge of the seat and arched his back, pushing upward against the apex of her thighs. Electricity lanced through her. He thrust both hands beneath her sweater and flattened them against her back, pressing her breasts to his chest, a most unsatisfactory arrangement, as far as she was concerned, and yet one that he seemed unwilling to rectify until she pushed her hands stubbornly against his chest.

He growled a complaint as she pulled her mouth from his, but when she grabbed at the hem of her sweater, he leaped to help her get it off, and when it was gone, he reached around her for the hook of her bra. She raked the straps over her shoulders herself and, holding his gaze with hers, let it fall away as she settled once more onto his lap and slowly leaned forward. He reached up and tangled his hands in her hair, pulling her down to him.

The first shock of skin against skin took her breath away, and then the spreading warmth of her breasts as she pressed them against his chest had her gasping and dragging in great gulps of air, until his mouth found hers, fastened and pulled her into him, so that she could no longer tell where he left off and she began. His hands dropped down to knead the bare skin of her back, imparting warmth and desire and an exquisite sense of belonging somewhere and to someone at last, even if it was only for the moment. Her tongue danced with his in a sensuous ballet of sliding, parrying thrusts, while her wandering hands gave his permission to roam.

Their every movement spread tingling, burning awareness that pooled in the pit of her belly. Bubbling, liquid desire. Heaven and hell in one all-encompassing moment. He found the heavy swells of her breasts and lifted them, cupped them, stroked them to throbbing peaks until she thrust against him, quivering and seeking hotter, more intense heat. He wrapped her in his arms and tried to crush her into the pores of his skin, and she willingly let him try, so much so that it was some time before she realized that he was slowly, inexorably pulling away.

When finally his hands settled lightly at her waist and he laid his head back against the seat to catch his breath, she knew that it was over. She flipped her hair out of her face and drew back, her forearms resting atop his shoulders, to speak a question with her eyes.

Sighing, he smoothed her hair with his hands. ''When

we make love,'' he explained huskily, ''it will be just that, love and nothing else.''

She knew what he was telling her. She might be willing, finally, to just feel alive again, but he needed more. She stroked her fingertips against his temple and answered him as honestly as she could. ''I can't promise you that.''

''I know,'' he said, ''not yet.''

''Maybe never.''

''And maybe tomorrow,'' he said, ''if you have the courage.''

Courage. How long had it been since she'd been willing to take the slightest risk, to chance the smallest pain? But even the most craven of cowards had to begin somewhere. She knew suddenly that if she had the merest chance of accepting what he tried so valiantly to give, she had to begin now. But not with him. She had left too much undone and unrisked before she'd met him. It was time to go back and take the paths she had rejected before. Then maybe she could work her way back to Morgan.

''I'm going to spend Thanksgiving with my family,'' she said suddenly.

If he was surprised, he gave no indication of it. Instead he smoothed his hands up her back and said, ''We'll miss you, Pop and I. I'll miss you. I'll always miss you.''

His kiss, this time, was reassuring and supportive, with only a hint of the passion he had just shown her. It made it all right, somehow, that she was sitting half naked astride his lap in a truck that wasn't quite as far off the road as it should have been. He helped her dress, hooking up her bra and pulling her sweater over her head before tugging on his own T-shirt and jacket. Only when they were fully clothed again did she slide off his lap and twist into her own seat. He stayed beside her, smoothing her hair with his hands and smiling, his gaze moving over her leisurely, admiringly, until she began to blush and then to laugh because she seemed to have it backward.

That was the trouble with her. She seemed to get so much backward, like being an adult when she should have been an adolescent and vice versa or becoming pregnant before she realized how deeply she wanted a child and pushing away everyone she most needed and wanted at the very moment that the need was most acute. She had a lot to get right, and she wasn't sure where or what she would be after the attempt, but she knew now that she was going to try. She knew now that remembering meant more than she'd believed. She wanted—and Jeremy deserved—all of it, the good and the bad, the joy and the pain. That's what she had to find a way to hold on to. She just didn't know yet if she could do it and hold on to Morgan, too.

Chapter Seven

It was difficult, more difficult than she had even imagined. Her parents wept when they saw her. Troy and May, who had driven up to Kansas City from their home in Springfield, were entirely too cheerful and insisted on knowing why Morgan hadn't come with her. She had to explain to everyone about Morgan. He was her landlord, okay, her friend. She didn't know herself if he was anything more than that. Privately, she replayed that episode in the truck at the side of the road over and over in her mind, marveling that she'd had the courage to do such a thing, wondering if he was thinking about it, too. What did it mean, that moment? Ultimately, did it really mean anything?

After Thanksgiving dinner, her mother and father wanted her to visit Jeremy's grave with them, but she couldn't do it. She hadn't done it since the day they'd buried him. After they left, her younger sister Cayla, a schoolteacher who had not yet married, scolded her for being selfish and maudlin and ungrateful. Troy had defended her, pointing out to Cayla that she couldn't possibly understand what it meant to love or lose a child. But

Cayla's condemnation hurt—and made her think. In the end she followed her parents to the cemetery and stood with them sobbing over Jeremy's grave. They spent the remainder of the evening looking at photographs and talking about him. It was sometimes funny and sometimes heartbreaking. Cayla, no longer cowed by Troy's lecture, pronounced the whole thing macabre, but Denise suspected that her little sister was in denial, and she wondered silently if her own experience with marriage and Jeremy's loss had anything to do with Cayla's defensiveness and the fact that she had never married. Of course, at twenty-eight Cayla was young yet. To Denise, Cayla seemed decades younger than her own thirty-five years.

Or was it that Denise felt decades older than her true age?

Denise spent the night in her old room in her parents' house, then made ready to return home to Jasper after breakfast the next day. Leaving was surprisingly painless, despite the need to sedate Smithson and wrestle him into his carrier. He'd been his usual prickly self all during the holiday, but she had forgiven him his standoffishness when he'd curled up next to her at night, as if sensing that she needed his warmth. When it was time to go, her parents hugged her and thanked her for coming. Nothing more was said about Jeremy, and no one suggested that she decide where to spend the Christmas holidays just then. Having taken her leave of her siblings the night before, Denise simply got into the car and started off. She headed south, but on the edge of the city limits she turned around and went back.

She drove past the turnoff to her parents' house and then took herself over the state line into Kansas and finally to the place where she and Jeremy had lived those last precious years together. The small frame house was gone, as were all the others that had comprised the block, to make way for an office building and parking garage. She hadn't

known that it was gone, but it seemed appropriate somehow. If Jeremy couldn't live there, why should anyone
else? She drove to the park where they'd spent so many
hours. The swings and merry-go-rounds had been freshly
painted and some picnic tables and new water fountains
had been installed. She parked the car at the curb, got out
and sat at one of the tables under the leafless trees, and
saw Jeremy again, running and laughing, touching the sky
with his feet as she pushed him in the swing, bawling when
she cleaned the knee he'd skinned on the slide. She saw
him dirty and smiling and happy with his friends. Finally,
she rose and went back to the car. She had one more stop
to make.

The intersection where Jeremy and his friends had been
hit by a van with faulty brakes had been changed, too. A
traffic light had been erected where only a stop sign had
stood before. A crosswalk had been drawn, and a bus stop
had been added. Absolutely no clue remained to alert a
busy world that once a precious little boy had died in the
middle of the street. Denise sat on the bench at the bus
stop dabbing at her tears with a crumpled tissue. A kindly
middle-aged black woman joined her and asked if anything
was wrong. Denise found herself explaining haltingly how
Jeremy had died. The woman had lost a grown daughter
at the hands of an abusive lover. The bus came and went.
Their stories told, the two embraced and parted with smiles
of commiseration. Denise had not even asked her name or
told her own, but she had faced a demon that day and
helped another woman face her own, the demon of sense-
less loss.

It was late in the evening before Denise arrived, exhausted, at the apartment. Smithson was awake and restless
and demanding to be let out of his carrier. As she sat the
carrier on the ground in front of the apartment and put the
key in the lock, she noticed that Morgan and a tall, dark-
haired young man were sitting on the porch of his house

sipping cups of what Denise took to be coffee. She felt raw, vulnerable, too much so for a meeting with Morgan Holt, but when he rose and called out to her, she left the carrier where it was and walked over to say hello and be introduced to Radley.

Both were wearing heavy sweaters over turtlenecks and jeans, but though they were dressed alike Morgan's son did not particularly resemble him. His features were too narrow, his hair too dark, but he had the vibrant blue eyes bequeathed to him by his father and grandfather. Radley smiled and nodded his head almost shyly when introduced to her.

"Care to join us for a cup of tea?" Morgan asked.

She lifted her eyebrows at that. Morgan Holt did not strike her as the sort of man to drink hot tea. Seeing her reaction, Radley laughed and explained, "I still haven't learned to drink coffee myself, and it's too chilly out for cold drinks, but I always enjoy a cup of tea. My grandmother taught me to drink it when I was kid."

"I used to drink tea with my grandmother," Denise told him.

"Which brings us back to my original question," Morgan said smoothly, holding his cup aloft. "Care to join us?"

Denise shook her head, but before she could explain that she wanted nothing with caffeine for fear it would interfere with badly needed sleep, Radley said, "We were just talking about indulging in something a little stronger. Maybe you'd like to join us for a real drink."

Denise remembered all too well what had happened the last time she and Morgan Holt had partaken of "real drink" together and flatly refused. "No. No, thank you. I have to see to my cat and unpack and… Well, I wouldn't want to intrude. Besides," she added quickly, reading protest in Morgan's eyes. "I'm tired."

Protest softened to compassion. "Rough trip?"

She nodded. "But rewarding."

He smiled. "Good."

"And your own holiday?"

"Fine." He frowned and shrugged. "Dad didn't quite seem himself." He smiled again. "But Radley was here, and that made all the difference. We had sort of an all-male Thanksgiving."

"Mom freaked," Radley said matter-of-factly, "but it was kind of fun, Grandpa, Dad and me."

Denise didn't know what to say to that, and apparently neither did Morgan, whose smile grew lame. In the midst of the silence, Reiver got up from his place on the welcome mat, stretched, yawned and padded down the steps. Denise quickly looked away from the sight of the big dog lifting his leg to relieve himself on the shrubbery that grew around the foundation of the house.

She cleared her throat, pretending that she wasn't embarrassed. "Well, I'll just say good-night now. You two enjoy your evening."

Both Morgan and Radley were holding in chuckles. Morgan did a commendable job of straightening his face and said, "I'll walk you to your door."

She bit her lip to keep from pointing out the obvious, that it was hardly necessary, given that her door was within plain sight. He came down the steps and took her arm, sliding his hand up into the curve of her elbow, then down the length of her arm until his big hand closed lightly around it just above her wrist. The contact was electric in the extreme. It was all she could do to keep from flinching as he turned her away from the porch.

"Oh, nice to meet you, Radley," she said over her shoulder, completely as an afterthought.

He was grinning like the proverbial cat who ate the canary. "Same here, Denise, er, Ms. Jenkins."

She opened her mouth to tell him that he could use her given name if he liked, but just then Morgan's hand slid over her wrist, bringing it palm to palm with her own. His long, strong fingers curled around hers. She swallowed the words, her breath catching in her chest. He led her along the walk. They were four or five yards from her front door when he said, "Are you okay?"

She nodded, grateful for something upon which to fix her thoughts. "I'm more tired than anything else. It was…a difficult trip." In some far corner of her mind, she recognized the sound of Smithson rattling the gate of his carrier, but it seemed remote, incidental. Morgan drew her to a halt and took both her hands in his.

"Listen, Rad and I have had a good visit. He won't mind if I slip off to spend a few hours with you. Maybe you need to talk and—"

"No." She shook her head. "Morgan, all I want right now is a long, hot soak in the tub, followed by bed."

His mouth quirked up in one corner. "Sounds great to me."

Heat diffused her. The memory, startlingly vibrant, of his hands on her bare breasts swept through her. It was as if time replayed that one clear instant of sensation. It was relived, slowly, minutely, completely, losing nothing in memory, revealing everything, most especially how very much she wanted to be with him. The sharpness and clarity of it frightened her. It was too real, too certain. She couldn't protect herself, couldn't think.

Suddenly Reiver's angry, frantic barking yanked her back to herself. In one searing flash of understanding, she realized that the big dog had wandered close to Smithson's carrier and a battle royale had been engaged despite the cage's gate between them. She didn't need to hear Smithson's threatening hisses to know that hostilities were about to escalate. She yanked her hands free of Morgan's and ran for the carrier. Just before she got there, the carrier's door came unlatched and Smithson bolted. For one awful instant, she feared that Reiver was going to tear her stupid,

prickly cat limb from limb, but Morgan had run after Denise and called Reiver to heel, which didn't stop the great
brute from snarling at poor Smithson, who shot off into
the night like a bolt of feline lightning.

Denise watched, openmouthed, as the cat literally vanished. It seemed like the worst kind of betrayal and aban-
donment given everything that she'd put up with and done
for that cat. And she knew suddenly who was to blame.
She rounded on him, irrational in her protective shield of
anger.

"Damn you, Morgan, you've as good as killed my cat!"

He gaped at her. "I what?"

"He's never been outside before! He's a house cat, Morgan! He only has his back claws. He can't even protect
himself!"

"Could've fooled me." This came from Radley, who
had loped down to the scene of the crime, so to speak, to
comfort Reiver, as if that great, slobbering beast needed or
deserved it. Denise turned a look of such venom on Radley
that he literally blanched, his eyes growing wide. She
switched her gaze to Morgan again, ready and willing to
take out her dismay on him.

"Your dog attacked my poor cat!"

"Come on, Denise, I know you're upset, but—"

"Don't you dare defend that monster! Smithson was in
his carrier!"

"There's a natural anathema between cats and dogs, you
know that. Reiver only—"

"He ought to be put down!" she cried. "And if he's
killed my cat, he will be! I'll see to it! Oh, blast!" She
stomped her foot as anger gave way to tears. Morgan
reached out with both arms, but she knew that if she fell
into them now she would be utterly lost. She was just too
vulnerable, too confused. She shook her head, backing
away. "I want my cat," she said plaintively. "You lost

my c-cat!'' She whirled away and yanked open the apartment door.

"Denise!"

She yanked it shut again, finding a glimmer of satisfaction in the bang as it slammed closed. She heard the curse words that Morgan spat and the uncertainty in Radley's voice as he said, "Dad? What do we do, Dad?"

"Lock up that dog!" Morgan ordered. "Then find that damned cat!"

Denise leaned against the closed door and started to sob, and she didn't even know why, really. She was easily as irritated with Smithson as the rest of the world, and yet she felt that she had lost everything, including her peace of mind, perhaps even her place in the world. She left the bags in the car and the carrier on the doorstep and climbed the stairs in the dark to fall fully clothed into bed, her relaxing bath—and her disturbing response to Morgan Holt's touch—forgotten.

She hadn't expected to fall asleep, but the difficulty with which she pulled herself to consciousness, in answer to the pounding inside her head, testified clearly to her state of unconsciousness. When she got nearer the surface, she realized the pounding was not inside her head but outside, and finally she realized that someone was knocking at her door. Groaning, she sat up and swung her legs off the side of the bed. She felt as if she'd been pummeled. Every muscle was sore, but she got to her feet and switched on a light. She was still wearing her all-weather coat and shoes, and she didn't see any reason to take them off now. She made herself go down the stairs to the entry, where she flipped on the overhead light. The knocking stopped. She reached for the bolt and realized that she hadn't even thrown it. Worse, when she pushed open the door, she heard the jangle of the keys she'd left in the outside lock. Radley Holt stood uncertainly on her doorstep, a live

towel clutched against his chest. The towel roiled and
hissed.

"My cat!"

"Yes, ma'am," he said ruefully and stepped up into the
entry, awkwardly clutching the moving towel and managing to pull the door closed behind him at the same time.
With the door safely closed, he extended the cat, towel and
all. Denise was absurdly happy, but when she reached out
to take hold of the cat, Smithson hissed, spat, and sunk his
teeth into the fleshy part of her hand between her thumb
and forefinger. Denise yelped and yanked her hands back.
Smithson leaped down and disappeared into the kitchen,
leaving Denise to nurse her hand and glance, embarrassed,
at Radley. He smiled understandingly.

"Got me, too. I don't think he much liked his foray into
the big wide world."

"He bit you? Oh, I'm so sorry, Radley. It's just that
he's not used to being outside and—" But, of course, it
wasn't just that the cat wasn't used to being outside. He
was prickly at the best of times.

Something banged against the door, and it bumped open,
jostling Radley out of the way. Morgan came in with her
overnight case and the cat carrier. He didn't so much as
look at her before carrying both into the living room and
putting them down, tossing her keys onto the coffee table.
He came back into the foyer and laid a hand on Radley's
shoulder. "Come on. I'll buy you that drink we talked
about."

Radley nodded, shot a look at Denise and went out,
pushing the door behind him. Denise wasted no time grabbing the opportunity to apologize. "Morgan, I'm sorry."

He nodded, shrugged, lifted his hands palm up in a gesture of helplessness. "Right. Listen, you need some sleep,
and I need…" He shook his head. "What I don't need is
to be cast as the bad guy again. I mean, I won't live like
that again, Denise, where everything that goes wrong is all

my fault, no matter how bizarre or unpredictable or remote." He put his hands to his hips and bowed his head, breathing deeply. She realized then how badly her unjustified accusations had hurt him.

"I'm so sorry. I had no right to blame you. I..." She put a hand to her head. "I'm so confused."

"Yeah, well, that makes two of us. Look, I gotta go. Rad's waiting."

She nodded. He opened the door and stepped outside. "Thanks for—" he waved a hand in dismissal and walked away "—everything," she finished softly. Carefully, she pulled the door closed and set the bolt. She could hear Smithson crunching cat food in the kitchen, and for a moment resentment flared. But the truth was that no one and nothing was to blame but herself. She had lashed out unfairly, and clearly Morgan had had enough of that in his life. Who could blame him if he kept his distance after this? Maybe it would be best if he did. Best for him, anyway.

She tore her thoughts away from Morgan and carried her bag upstairs where she unpacked it and put it away. That done, she sat on the side of the bed and considered what to do next. She still felt that she could sleep about forty-eight hours straight, but she was oddly reluctant to crawl back into the bed. Despite her exhaustion, she was keyed up, restless. She decided to take that long, hot bath she'd been wanting.

Forty minutes later she emerged from the steam-filled bathroom. Her hair was piled up loosely on top of her head, and she wore a long, soft gown of brushed cotton and her warmest terry-cloth robe and matching slippers. Unfortunately, rather than being relaxed and sleepy, she felt invigorated. She went downstairs, made herself a snack and a cup of cocoa, and settled on the sofa in the living room, intending to watch a little late-night television. Five minutes into the late movie, the cable went out. A quarter-hour later, she gave up and switched it off, then took down a favorite book and prepared to be engrossed. But it was too quiet, too…lonely. She thought of Morgan and Radley sitting in some cozy, candlelit bar somewhere, quaffing beers and laughing together, probably about what an idiot she was. She put down the book and got up to turn on the stereo.

What she needed was some soothing music. She laid her head back and let the beauty of Brahms wash over her. Smithson apparently decided that he needed a lap, for he suddenly leaped into hers, sending her bolt upright, one brow arching. "So you've decided you want a snuggle, have you?"

The cat ignored her, grooming his paws and whiskers with haughty concentration. It wouldn't do her any good, she knew, to scold, and besides, what did she have except this hateful old cat? Suddenly, the emptiness of her own life threatened to devour her, and something told her that it would unless she found the courage to love again. But how could she? How could she risk losing someone dear to her again? She couldn't survive that kind of devastation again. She couldn't. And yet, somehow, she couldn't quite face the idea of spending her life alone, either. Bone-deep sadness settled over her, sadness so poignant it was beyond tears.

After a few minutes Smithson hopped down and went on his way, complacently superior. Denise shook her head ruefully, got up and switched off the stereo and climbed the stairs to bed.

She lay in the darkness, weary to the soul but wide-awake. She thought of all that had happened over the holiday and was thankful that she had finally faced the ghosts of her past life. The question now was how to face the future. She was still pondering that question when she heard laughter in the distance. Gladly, she rose, pulled on her robe and went to the window. Pushing aside the curtains, she gazed down into a still, cold night. Movement at the very edge of her vision made her turn her head. There beneath the streetlight on the corner were Morgan and Rad, their arms thrown about each other's shoulders, their breath frosting the air as they laughed and spoke.

It quickly became obvious that they were rip-roaring drunk. She lost sight of them as they lurched into deep shadow, but soon they tumbled out on the other side, stumbling and careening and falling to roll on the grass. A brief wrestling match ensued, ending when Morgan wound up with a hammerlock on Radley's coat, Radley slipping away to hoot and point and tease. Laughing, Morgan chased him into the house. She watched for a long time afterward, but they didn't come out again. Eventually, the lights in the house winked off one by one. Denise went back to her own, now cold bed and settled down once more. Her final thought as she drifted at last into desperately needed slumber was that Morgan had brought her Danish and coffee when she'd been hungover—and she had rejected it out of hand.

It was Radley who let her in the next morning.

"Hi. Cat okay?"

She gave him a small, apologetic smile. "The cat's fine. I, um, don't think I thanked you properly for bringing him home to me."

He shrugged. "No sweat. It wasn't like he could get up a tree or anything. Besides, it was Dad who actually caught him."

"Yes, well, is your father in?"

Radley seemed to hesitate, his smile a fraction too slow. "Yeah, he's here. Um, I was just leaving, though. I have an errand to run." He reached for a coat hanging on a hook on the hall tree and shrugged into it, shouting, "Dad! Denise is here!" He shot her an apologetic grimace. "Ms. Jenkins, that is."

"Denise will do just fine," she told him. Morgan stepped out into the entry hall. Radley beat a hasty retreat, flipping his father a wave and slipping out the door. Morgan frowned, but whether it was because of her or Radley, Denise didn't know. She smiled gamely. "Hi. I wanted to thank you again and—"

"Morgan?" Denise broke off as a tall, slender, shockingly attractive woman stepped into the hallway.

Morgan's chin came up, and he split a wary glance between Denise and the other woman. She was perfectly groomed, her soft blond hair twisted up in a sleek, sophisticated style. Large, almond-shaped eyes of a startling green coolly took her measure and seemed to find her wanting. Denise suddenly felt under dressed in her half boots, dark corduroy jeans, turtleneck and classic wool jacket, her dark hair pulled back into a simple ponytail. The other woman wore black pleated slacks, heels, a cream-colored silk blouse and a flared, houndstooth jacket, clearly a designer piece. Her makeup was perfect, her nails long and red. The leather belt cinched at her waist left no doubt as to its trim circumference. The woman's gaze dismissed Denise as unimportant and fixed possessively on Morgan.

"Are we through here?"

"Uh, no."

"I didn't think so." She folded her arms in a gesture both smug and elegant.

Denise kept waiting for Morgan to introduce her. Instead, he bounced glances off every object in the room except her, finally saying to the woman at his elbow, "I'll only be a minute, Belinda. This is business."

Belinda sniffed through her exquisitely narrow, straight nose and disappeared back the way she'd come. Morgan cleared his throat and walked forward, saying, "This is business, isn't it, Denise? I mean, all things considered, it could hardly be anything else."

Her heart dropped to the soles of her feet. He was seeing someone else then. He'd given up on her. Well, she had no one to blame but herself. She took a deep breath, surprised that it hurt, that her chest felt so tight and constricted. She managed a nod. "Ah, the c-cable's out in my apartment."

"Really? I haven't heard from any of the other tenants about it. Are you sure you're equipment is in working order?"

"No. No, I'm not. Th-that's why I've called for a repairman." She drew another deep breath, careful to keep her gaze targeted just below his chin. "The thing is, he can't come until M-Monday. I was hoping you... I was hoping you would let him in."

He stood there for a moment, his hands on his hips, and she really thought that he was going to refuse. But then he nodded. "Sure. No problem. What time?"

She shrugged. "B-before noon. Sorry I can't be more precise."

"Okay." Just that. Nothing more.

Denise tried to think for several moments what her reply to that should be, but in the end she could do no more than mutter her thanks and get out of there. She practically ran back to the apartment, where she hadn't a blessed thing to do. Not that she was capable of any rational action just then. She was breathless, stunned. In shock. It wasn't even so much that Morgan was seeing someone else, someone perfect and elegant and very sure about what she wanted— Denise didn't stop to think how she knew that. No, it was how much it hurt. It was the depth of the pain. Suddenly she knew that there were more ways to lose someone than she'd ever guessed, and telling herself that she shouldn't, couldn't, care was not adequate protection. Perhaps no such protection existed. Perhaps the human heart made its own rules, and the human intellect was powerless against it. Which left her right where she'd always been, with too much of absolutely nothing.

Morgan closed the door behind Belinda and put both hands to his temples. He said a silent prayer of thanks for the good Dr. Isaiah, who had married his ex and carried her off to Little Rock, from which she usually confined her know-it-all demands to long-distance telephoning. Radley's decision to bypass the usual Thanksgiving at her palatial home in the country club section of the state capitol had prompted his mother to make the drive up from Little Rock in order to verbally tear a strip off both their hides. Only Rad had fled the worst of it, the rat, leaving Morgan to listen with half an ear while she told him, with great conviction, how pathetic he was as a father. She blamed him for everything from Rad's inability to settle on a career choice to her cook's inability to prepare a perfect turkey. She and the doctor had had friends in—influential people, of course—and she had been forced to explain to them that her own son had chosen to spend this most precious of family holidays with his father and grandfather! He'd had a hard time not laughing at that.

But he didn't feel like laughing now. His head was pounding, the effect of too much alcohol, no doubt, too much alcohol and too much Belinda—but too little Denise. He'd really thought that she was making progress, that her trip back home would somehow put to rest some of the unresolved issues that seemed to surround her son's death and hold her back from a loving relationship. With him. He'd been so sure that he was right for her and vice versa. When she'd blamed him for her stupid cat getting out of its carrier, he'd felt a horrid chill, a terrible sense of déjà vu. He hadn't expected that from her. It was just the sort of thing he'd expect of Belinda, though. And that was the problem. He couldn't go through that again, being blamed for everything under the sun that displeased her, never be-

ing able to get it right, wanting so badly and failing so
miserably to make her happy.

On the other hand, he'd just been through a solid hour
of Belinda's absurd accusations, and it hadn't affected him
in any way like that one moment of absurdity with Denise
last night had. Then, too, she had apologized—just as soon
as she'd calmed down. Belinda, conversely, could insult
him for hours on end without ever getting visibly upset. It
was second nature to her, like buying the most expensive
of everything or bleaching her hair. Besides, he'd stopped
loving Belinda long ago, or rather, he had stopped trying
to love her. Somehow he didn't seem to have to try with
Denise. Almost from the moment he'd met her, he'd just
felt that they were right for each other. Unfortunately, she
didn't seem to feel the same way, and he had promised
himself years ago that he would not love a woman who
couldn't love him back. Not again.

He went into the kitchen and dug up a couple of aspirin,
slugging them back with a cold glass of milk. His stomach
rebelled, but after much grumbling settled down to digest
the much-needed analgesic. He heard Radley come in. No
doubt the rascal had just been waiting for his mother to
leave. Radley's boots clumped on the hardwood floor.

"Mother gone?"

"You know perfectly well that she is."

He didn't deny it. "You okay?"

"Your mother's been sinking her claws in me for
twenty-five long years. I've never died of it before."

"You've never had such a hangover before."

Morgan sent a confirming look over his shoulder. "And
won't have again."

"Famous last words."

"Naw, I'm too old for that nonsense. Don't know what
got into me last night."

"No? I'd say that was pretty obvious."

Morgan turned another look across his shoulder. "Growing up on me, are you?"

Radley shrugged and answered glumly, "Has to happen sometime."

"Better late than never, is that it?" Morgan chuckled. "Don't let your mother get to you. You just hang in. You'll come through fine."

Radley rubbed a finger along his nose. "I wasn't really thinking of Mother. I was thinking more of Grandpa—and you."

That had Morgan actually turning around to face his son. "How so, Rad?"

Radley was clearly uncomfortable, but he tried to put his feelings into words. "It's just that— I don't know. Thursday, Grandpa seemed…smaller than he used to be. I mean, it's like he wasn't quite all here, you know? And it seemed to me that you kept wandering off on your own, too, like…well, like me and Grandpa weren't quite enough for you anymore."

"Oh, Rad, no. Son, if I gave you the impression—"

"Hey, I'm not feeling sorry for myself, and I'm not criticizing. I'm just saying that for the first time, I felt like the one who was wholly and completely with it. You know?"

Morgan's mouth quirked, but he successfully forestalled an actual grin. "Yeah, I think I do."

Rad nodded, as if that acknowledgment of a common experience was everything to him. "Okay, so can I ask you something, just between us men?"

"Ask away."

"What happened with Denise? Was Mother awful to her?"

Morgan carefully shook his head. "Your mother ignored her."

"So is it okay with you guys, then?"

Morgan opened his mouth to make light of it and say

that all was fine, but the grown-up Rad deserved better. He ran a hand over his head. At least his hair no longer hurt, he thought ruefully and sighed. "I don't know, Rad. Denise is...well, she's...wounded." He put a hand to the back of his neck. "It's complicated. She had a son, too, but he died unexpectedly, and she can't seem to get over it. Not that I blame her, you understand. I can only imagine what it would have done to me—what it would still do to me—to lose you like that."

"What about the boy's dad?" Radley wanted to know.

"He wasn't part of their lives. He didn't want kids, so when Denise came up pregnant, he left her."

"What a jerk!"

Privately Morgan agreed. Publicly he believed in not judging. "The thing is, she just can't seem to get past it."

"So what are you going to do?" Radley asked, obviously not so grown-up that he didn't expect Dad to come up with all the answers.

Morgan closed his eyes. "I don't know. I'm not sure there's anything I can do."

"Huh." It was clearly an unfamiliar concept to Radley but an acceptable one. "Bummer," he said. Then he turned and walked out of the room.

"Bummer," Morgan echoed faintly. Yeah, that about summed it up. Sometimes life was just a bummer.

Chapter Eight

Denise left Chuck's office and strode down the corridor toward her own, her composure in place, her expression bland, despite the fact that she felt like shouting in celebration. Jenkins will be handling all new negotiations. From now on everything has to be run by her. She smiled. Jenkins. Not Dennis, not even Denise, but Jenkins. She was an official member of the Good Old Boys club. She had, finally, passed muster. And Chuck hadn't even made the usual sexist jokes at her expense. He'd asked briefly about her holiday and cracked that Morgan would never again play racquetball in this town because no one with any sense wanted his brains beat out by a hotdog player. Then, as the meeting was breaking up, Chuck had calmly, offhandedly announced that some executive realignment was in order. Henceforth, Jenkins would be titled Director of Contract Development and all contract goals were to be set and/or approved by her office, to which end she would be allowed to hire not one and not two but three assistants. To her surprise her peers had applauded her to a man.

She felt exultant in a way that she hadn't in… She

stopped to consider. The last time she'd felt like this was when she'd been admitted to the school of business Master's program. So long ago. So very long ago. Wondering why that was, she continued down the hall and turned the corner.

"Betty, we have work to do," she announced, suddenly bursting at the seams to tell someone. Betty stood up, one hand covering the mouthpiece of the telephone receiver, worry wrinkling her normally smooth forehead.

"It's a Radley Holt, Ms. Jenkins. He says there's an emergency."

Denise literally staggered to a halt, her heart dropping. Had something happened to Morgan? A picture of Jeremy's small, broken body flashed before her mind's eye, and then it was Morgan whom she saw lying lifeless and bloody. Her knees buckled. She saved herself only by lunging toward the desk and grabbing at the phone. And yet, in that instant in which she lifted the telephone receiver to her ear she experienced one of those rare moments of clarity that comes with revelation.

Once before she had experienced such an epiphany. It had occurred in that moment after the doctor had told her that she was pregnant and the back of her head had hit the wall behind her chair. In that moment of shock she had suddenly understood that the child she had not known existed only a moment before was the most important thing in her life. Just as she knew now that Morgan Holt was far dearer, far more important and much closer to the center of her heart than she had ever suspected. She could not bear to lose him. He wasn't even hers, and she could not bear the thought of losing him. She gripped the phone with every ounce of physical strength that she possessed.

"Rad?"

"Denise! It's Gran'pa Ben! They came for Dad, and he went up to the cabin with them. He was crying! I haven't ever seen him so upset. I think he needs us—you. Will you come?''

Relief gave way to deep, sorrowful concern. Ben needed Morgan, and Morgan needed her. That could mean only one thing. She pushed the thought of death away and concentrated on the most immediate concern. ''Where are you?''

''Downstairs in the lobby.''

''I'll be right there.''

She set the receiver in its cradle. Betty had gone into her office to get her purse. She held it out to Denise with a blatant look of compassion. ''Is there anything I can do?''

It rocked Denise to feel the gentle waves of concern and sympathy emanating from the secretary from whom she had maintained such personal distance. She found herself gripping not only her purse but Betty's hand. ''Thanks. Just batten down the hatches and tell anyone who needs to know that I've been called away by a personal emergency.''

''I hope it isn't too bad,'' Betty said.

Denise smiled wanly. ''Me, too.'' Then she pushed away from the desk and strode rapidly toward the elevators.

Radley was pacing the floor in front of the security desk. His eyes rounded when he spotted her coming toward him. She felt his mild shock at the sight of her ''work persona.'' She knew that her appearance said ''All business'' and ''All woman'' at the same time. Because of today's meeting she had carefully selected the black heels and stockings, the short, slender, red skirt and the fitted, collarless, winter-white jacket that closed all the way to the neck with big black buttons. Her accessories included a black handbag, a watch with a black leather band and black pearls for her earlobes. She knew that her tone was almost amused despite her worry when she asked, "Should we take time for me to change, do you think?"

He shook his head. "We may be too late already."

He took her arm and turned, leading her in swift strides toward the door. "It's that bad, then?"

The gaze he turned to her was bleak. "I think Ben's dying."

"I was afraid of that." She briefly closed her eyes. Could she do this? She wouldn't be much use to Morgan if she fell apart. Morgan. Ben was his father. He was the one entitled to fall apart, and Rad had said that he was crying. She lifted her chin and mentally squared her shoulders. She would not let him down. Suddenly the most important thing in her world was being there for Morgan. She quickened her stride.

Radley was driving Morgan's truck. He explained as she climbed up into the cab that a neighbor of Ben's had come for Morgan, and that he, Radley, had promised to follow as soon as he'd called for an ambulance and his Aunt Delia. Morgan had asked him to call Denise as well. He had decided on his own to ask her to go with him. She reached across the cab and squeezed his hand.

"Thank you."

"I just thought you could be there for Dad," he said, his voice breaking.

Denise nodded understandingly and buckled her seat belt.

It was a harrowing trip. Radley's driving at times frightened her, and yet every moment was filled with the greater worry that they wouldn't get to the cabin in time. Gray clouds hovered overhead, adding the threat of rain to a deepening sense of desperation. The drive seemed to take forever. By the time they reached the rutted trail that led up to the cabin, Denise's nails had poked deep creases into her palms, and her teeth had worried the inside edge of her lower lip until it was bloody.

They pulled up in the yard to find that an ambulance had been backed in to the very edge of the rickety porch, but the attendants were standing beside it, arms folded or hands in their pockets, heads together in quiet conversation as if uncertain what they should be doing at the moment. An old pickup truck, its once-red paint faded to a dusty pink, mottled with the gray of bare metal and the orange of rust, was parked at an angle on the steep hillside, a basketball-size rock guarding one rear wheel. A grizzled gentleman in overalls, coat and slouch hat sat on the bumper puffing a pipe. Radley parked his father's truck next to the ambulance and baled out, going straight to the farmer with the pipe. Denise checked the urge to go right to the house and followed. The old man got up and extended his hand to Radley.

"Grady, what's going on?" Radley demanded.

The old man shook his head and motioned with his pipe. "Amb'lance got here 'bout five minutes ago, but Ben refuses to leave. Says he's dying at home. Morg's in there with him now."

Denise had turned and was already heading up toward the house, her heels sinking into the soft loam of the hillside. Radley caught up and, with his arm around her waist, helped her manage the last few yards. She hurried across the porch and pushed open the door without bothering to knock, Radley right on her heels.

A low, raspy chuckle called her toward the far corner of the room. Morgan sat in a dining chair pulled up to the side of the small double bed tucked beneath the open stairway, his back to them. The click of her heels as she hurried across the plank floor did not induce him to turn away from the man on the bed, and as she drew near, she understood why.

Ben's face was unnaturally pale, the skin beneath his eyes and around his mouth an oxygen-depleted blue. The gnarled hand that lay between both of Morgan's was swollen and purplish, a clear indication of severe circulatory problems. His breathing was slow and labored, his eyes closed in exhaustion. He was fully dressed right down to his boots, which, like one shirtsleeve and jeaned leg, were muddy. Apparently he had taken a fall, but whether that had preceded the obvious health problems or vice versa, was not immediately obvious. Denise did not suppose that it mattered.

She stepped up behind Morgan and laid her hands gently upon his shoulders. He immediately lifted one shoulder and laid his cheek against her fingers in a kind of hug. "Look who's here, Pop," he cajoled softly, and Ben's blue-tinged eyelids struggled to lift. The eyes revealed were almost colorless and clearly blind. "It's Radley and Denise," Morgan supplied. To Denise and Radley he added as lightly as he could, "We've been reminiscing."

Ben's mouth curved into a smile. "Rad," he whispered.

Radley went down on one knee and laid his hand upon his grandfather's chest. "I'm here, Gran'pa."

"Fun...two us," Ben managed.

Radley gulped. "We sure did. We had lots of fun together."

"Good...boy," Ben said, but then he made as if to shake his head and corrected himself. "Man... Good...man. Proud...you."

Radley bowed his head, whispering, "I'm proud of you, too, Gran'pa, very proud."

Ben sighed, and his hand flexed in Morgan's. "Love you...son."

Denise felt Morgan struggling to make a calm reply. Finally he caught his breath and said, "I love you, too, Pop."

"D'ise," Ben slurred, his eyes closing again.

She swallowed down the lump in her throat and softly replied, "I'm here, Ben."

"Take care...my son."

For the life of her, she could do nothing more than nod and choke out the one word, "Yes."

Ben sighed again, and for a long moment lay so still that Denise feared the end had come, but then he coughed, just once, and gripped Morgan's hand tightly. His eyes opened, and he turned his head to look squarely into Morgan's face. "Tell Delia," he rasped, "that Ma came to meet me, just like I knew she would." He turned his head on the pillow, staring up at the ceiling. He smiled, and his hand left Morgan's to settle at his side on the bed. Then his eyes closed, and an instant later, he was gone.

It was as if some of the warmth had left the room, as if the world contained a little more space than it should despite the body lying peacefully upon the faded quilt atop the bed. Denise shook her head, wanting to deny what she could not doubt. She had seen death before. She could never forget the feel of it. Morgan, too, knew that his father had left them. His shoulders began to shake, and he slid off the edge of his chair onto his knees. Slowly he leaned across his father's body, his hands grasping handfuls of quilt and shirt as he tried to hold his father's essence with him just one moment longer.

Radley was the last to perceive that Ben was no longer with them. He stared aghast at his father's heaving shoulders and struggled up to his feet, crying, "Gran'pa? Gran'pa!" He backed away, and Denise feared for a moment that he would run, but when she reached out a hand to him, he turned tear-filled eyes to her and said shakily, "He's with Gran'ma now. That's what he wanted, and now they're together again."

Denise nodded, her own tears rolling down her cheeks, and gripped his hand tightly. They stood together, watching over Morgan as he grieved, letting the peace of this place and this moment settle over them. After a long while, Morgan raised his head. It took some little time after that for him to pull himself together, but finally he stood and gazed down at the body that seemed to shrink and grow colder with every passing moment. Radley pulled free of Denise's hand and walked to the door.

"I think you guys should come in and move him now," he told the EMTs waiting beside the ambulance. As they prepared to do just that, Denise stepped forward to stand at Morgan's side and slip an arm around his waist. He didn't look at her, but his arm came up and draped her shoulders, pulling her tight against him. He rubbed his free hand over his face and cleared his throat.

"Thank you for coming," he said huskily.

She laid her head in the hollow of his shoulder and looped her other arm lightly about his torso. "I had to," she whispered. "I didn't want to, but I had to."

"Yeah, I know just what you mean. Frankly, after everything you've been through, I wouldn't blame you if you stayed away."

"It's because of what I've been through that I had to come," she told him softly.

He said nothing to that, just stood staring down at his father's body. After a bit she said, "He looks so at peace."

"Yes." His hand came up and stroked the hair at her temples. "Was it that way with Jeremy? Was he at peace?"

She had to think about that, and something in her rebelled at the truth, but finally she found the strength to admit that it was the same. "He might have been sleeping," she said softly. "Except that I knew at first glance that he wasn't really there. That wasn't my little boy anymore. He was gone, and nothing I could do would bring him back again."

"That's the difference," Morgan said, turning so that she stood pressed against his chest. "I wouldn't bring Pop back even if I could, no matter how much I might want to."

She nodded understanding, whispering, "He's where he

wants to be. I believe Radley's right when he says that Ben
is with your mother now.''

Morgan lifted his chin and laid it atop her head. ''I believe it, too. He wanted us to believe it.''

She closed her eyes, trying not to say the words that had
formed in her mind. This moment was about Morgan, not
her. Yet, somehow the words found their own way out. ''I
wish someone was with Jeremy.''

''He's not alone,'' Morgan said with strong certainty.
''If he was before, he wouldn't be now, anyway. Pop
thought about him a lot, you know, ever since we told him.
I can see him now, looking out for this bright little boy
with a grubby face and a skinned knee. Pop would go
down on his haunches and push back his cap and say in
that slow voice of his, 'You must be Denise's boy. Your
mama sure loves and misses you, son.' Then he'd take
Jeremy by the hand, just the way he took yours that day,
and he'd say, 'Come and meet Ma now.' No, Jeremy's not
alone. Never will I believe Pop would forget him, even in
Paradise.''

Denise found herself smiling, despite the tears that
leaked from her eyes to wet the front of Morgan's sweatshirt. She felt as if she'd been crying forever and, oddly,
as if she would never cry again. In her mind's eye she saw
Jeremy walking away from her, his little hand snug in
Ben's strong, tough one. He was laughing and talking a
mile a minute and skipping about every third step, and in
her heart she knew that this, at last, was goodbye. She
closed her eyes and felt the peace of Morgan's steady
heartbeat against her cheek. Radley's voice brought her
head up and loosed Morgan's embrace.

''Dad, they're ready to take him now. I think you ought
to go outside.''

Morgan nodded and cleared his throat. ''All right, son.''

Together they walked through the door and slipped out
of it. Someone met them on the porch and shoved a clip-

board at Morgan. Resignedly, he filled in a few blanks, had a word or two with the attendant and signed his name at the bottom of the page. Radley could be heard inside giving directions about closing up the house and locating his grandfather's only suit. It seemed to Denise that he sounded at least a decade older than the frightened boy who had driven her here in such a panic. She remembered how his grandfather had told him of his pride in him and silently thanked Ben for that bit of wisdom.

Morgan walked her to the truck and lifted her up into the cab before scooting in next to her on the passenger side. He fastened her seat belt and then his own. When that was done, he settled back with a sigh. "What a day."

What a day, indeed! It occurred to her that she had news to share. "I ought to tell you, I got a promotion today."

He beamed a smile at her. "Did you? That's good news."

"Chuck mentioned you at the meeting," she went on. "Seems you're a real hustler on the racquetball court."

"Damn straight, and he would know, the weiner. I waxed his butt good."

She chuckled at that. He grinned, but it wasn't possible to sustain the lightened mood. The grin faded, and he turned tear-filled eyes upon her, his face rigid with the effort to remain straight.

"Thank you," he said softly. "Thank you for getting to know my dad and for being here now."

"I wouldn't have missed it for the world," she vowed, laying her head on his shoulder, "not a moment of it."

He laid his cheek against the top of her head. "Denise, about Belinda," he began, but then Radley appeared at the door of the truck, and Morgan straightened uncomfortably, falling silent. Radley climbed behind the wheel and buckled his belt.

"You okay, Dad?"

"As okay as I can be. I want to thank you for handling all that in there."

Radley cleared his throat. "Glad to be of help. Uh, I told them Smart and Blake Funeral Home."

Morgan put his head back and closed his eyes. "Fine. That's fine, son. Let's go home."

Radley started the truck, backed it around and got it headed down the slope to the paved road. Denise bit her lip, wanting badly to ask Morgan what he'd started to say about Belinda, but now was clearly not the time, and she wasn't absolutely certain that she wanted to hear what he had to say. He might have meant to warn her that Belinda would be around from now on. He might have been trying to tell her exactly what that would mean to their so-called friendship.

She felt his arm around her shoulders and sensed in that simple gesture a definite lack of the passion that had burned between them when last they'd traveled this road. Passion was not to be expected in a situation like this, of course, and yet its absence troubled her more than she liked to admit. She told herself to be content with giving comfort. She was the one Radley had called, after all, the one he was sure that his father needed at his side at a time like this. She didn't want to think about what might happen when Belinda showed up again, and surely she would if only to convey her condolences.

They were almost to Fayetteville when Radley shifted in his seat and said, "I didn't want to mention it earlier, but Aunt Delia was pretty upset when I called her."

Morgan sighed and lifted his head. "No surprise there."

"Yeah, well, I just thought I should warn you. She was screaming about how it was all your fault and everything. She even said you should've called her instead of me. I might not have been as nice as I should have."

"Don't worry about it," Morgan said tiredly. "We're all upset today."

"All the more reason for her to behave like a grown-up," Denise muttered, but if either of her companions heard her, he gave no indication.

Denise suggested that the guys drop her off at the office so she could pick up her car. Then she made them both promise to let her worry about dinner. People were pouring out of the building as she entered, and it occurred to her that she had never been a part of the daily exodus at quitting time simply because she usually left later than everyone else. Despite the promotion, she felt an odd stab of envy for all those satisfied people content to leave the job behind and hurry home to their loved ones. She thought of Morgan and the loss he'd suffered and had to literally force herself onto the only elevator going up. When she reached her office, it was to find Betty gone and Chuck going through the files stacked on her desk. He looked up sharply when she entered the room.

"Where the hell have you been?"

She felt a spurt of resentment. "I'm sure Betty told you that I had a personal emergency."

"Oh, really? A personal emergency on the heels of a personal triumph?" he asked skeptically. "Look, no one could fault you for wanting to celebrate, but not in the middle of a workday, for pity's sake! I thought you had better timing than that."

She walked to the desk and let her handbag drop with a thunk onto its corner. "Morgan's father died just over an hour ago."

He had the grace to look sheepish. "Oh, hey, I had no idea. B-but it's not like you're married to the guy or anything."

He might have stabbed her in the heart, so acute was the longing she felt. Married to Morgan Holt. Sweet heaven. She hadn't realized until this moment how very much she loved him. She gasped air. "I...I had to be with him. You don't know how close they were, Morgan and

Ben, how devoted. Morgan needs me now, a-and I'm going to be there for him no matter what.''

Chuck's surprise was evident in the sudden arching of both shaggy brows. "Well. What about work?''

"I'll take care of it. Somehow. Tonight I'll draw up an organizational chart for my new department and get Betty on it first thing tomorrow morning. The interviews can wait a few days—until after the funeral.''

He slid his hands into his pants pockets and rocked back on his heels. "What about current contracts? Dilbert's Dry Goods wants a last-minute change. Their rep called me today and—''

"They're trying an end run, Chuck. I've already told Dilbert's no, so he's gone around me to you, without bothering to inform you that his last gambit failed.'' She reached into the pile of folders on her desk and extracted the correct one. Flipping it open, she showed him the note she'd made concerning Dilbert's proposed change. He read through them quickly, and the last of the censure went out of his expression and tone.

"Hmm, pretty cheeky, if you ask me.'' After a moment he closed the file and laid it on top of the pile. "I admire a guy with audacity,'' he said, "but you gave him the right answer.'' He cleared his throat. "Want me to take care of it?''

She shook her head. "No, thanks. It'll have more impact coming from me. Not only will he know that you have agreed with me, he'll think twice about pulling this trick again.''

Chuck cleared his throat. "Won't hurt to add the new title after your name, either, will it?''

Denise smiled wanly. "No, it won't.''

He nodded and sidestepped toward the door. "Well, um, I'll let you…do whatever you came to do.''

"Thank you.'' She walked briskly around the desk and sat down as he moved toward the door. "Oh, and, um, if you need to reach me while I'm out, I'll be carrying my cell phone. I usually leave it in the car, but I'll have it on my person until this is over.''

He rubbed his hands together. ''Excellent. And, ah, give my sympathy to Morgan, please.''

To her surprise, he actually sounded sincere. ''I'll do that.''

''Maybe I'll send some flowers, too.''

She was thunderstruck. ''I... That would be nice.''

''Fine. That's what I'll do then.''

''Fine.''

''Okay. All right. Well...I'll see you.''

She nodded dumbly. He gave her a smart wave, turned on his heel and left her. She shook her head bemusedly. She must be more upset than she realized because for a moment there, Chuck Dayton had actually seemed human.

Morgan sighed and sat forward, cradling his head in his uplifted hands. He supposed that he should feel grateful for the numbness that seemed to encase him, but he couldn't seem to feel even that tepid emotion. It was strange and even a little frightening in a purely logical, objective fashion. Intellectually he knew that the numbness was a product of shock, and yet he couldn't quite reconcile that fact. He'd known so long that Ben was living on borrowed time that it didn't seem reasonable to experience shock when the end had finally come. So why was this lethargy binding him in place? Why couldn't he wrap his mind around the fact that his father was gone?

Denise carried flatware to the sink and began running water. He ought to help her, but he couldn't seem to find the energy. After all, she had provided dinner for him and Rad, a tasty carry-in Chinese that he hadn't been able to make himself eat. The cartons were safely stored away in the refrigerator, awaiting the moment his appetite returned.

The doorbell chimed and Radley got up to answer it.

Morgan felt not even mild curiosity about who might be calling, not that it mattered, for the voice in his hallway clearly identified itself only moments later. The tone, unsurprisingly, was angry, and yet he could not make himself sit upright to face his sister's wrath. He did manage to look up as she entered the kitchen and caught sight of his ex's smug face behind her, along with the apologetic grimace of his downtrodden brother-in-law, Howard.

Delia stomped into the room with all the outrage her diminutive size could muster. Her short, dark hair was, as always, expertly tousled, her large, expressive eyes—made a vibrant, electric blue with the aid of colored contact lenses—were meticulously made-up and snapping with indignation.

"My poor daddy!" she wailed. "I hope you're satisfied! You've as good as killed him yourself! Why wouldn't you listen to me? You've never been able to do the difficult thing, no matter how necessary! He shouldn't have been up there all alone, damn you! Why couldn't you just move him in here? God knows you have more than enough room!"

"That's enough."

Like everyone else, he had to look at Denise to be certain that it was she who had actually spoken.

"Who are you?" Delia demanded.

"Denise Jenkins."

"Oh, that's Morgan's little friend," Belinda sneered. "I told you about her, dear."

Morgan knew that if he'd been himself he'd have taken great offense at both the wording and tone of Belinda's statement. At the moment, however, he couldn't seem to find the energy.

Delia was fit enough, however. Never mind that it was her father who had died, too. She glared at Denise. "I'll thank you to stay out of this. You can't possibly know—"

"But I do," Denise interrupted flatly. "You're the one

who doesn't know what she's talking about. Ben lived as long as he did precisely because Morgan didn't force him down off that mountain."

"Why, you interfering little—"

Morgan knew that the battle was about to be joined, and yet he couldn't seem to make himself speak up. Thankfully, Radley pushed his way through the crowded doorway to lend his support.

"Denise is right, Aunt Delia," he asserted calmly. "Moving away from the cabin would have killed Gran'pa."

Deprived of the release of her anger, Delia opted for sympathy. Almost instantly huge tears welled in her eyes and trickled down her cheeks. "What would a boy like you know about it? He was my daddy, and I've lived with this awful fear for years, but would my Pollyannish brother do anything about it? Obviously putting my mind at rest never meant anything to him, and neither did our daddy's life!"

"That's unfair and you know it!" Denise exclaimed. Stepping close she laid her hands on the back of his chair. He knew that if he could just make himself sit upright again she would move her hands to his shoulders. But what difference would it make? Ben would still be gone, and Delia would still blame him for it. Morgan sighed again, and even that seemed pointless and futile. He wished absently that they'd all just go away and leave him alone. Listening required more energy than he possessed at the moment, but not listening required more.

"How dare you butt in like this?" Delia was demanding of Denise.

"Who do you think you are?" Belinda added supportively.

"What business is it of yours?" Denise snapped back.

"Delia is my best friend, I'll have you know! Ben was my father-in-law, and Radley—"

Radley shot an apologetic look at Denise and quickly stepped into the fray. "Uh, Denise, this is my mother."

He should have told her himself, Morgan reflected dully. Well, it couldn't be helped now. Not even the mingled sounds of shock and hurt in Denise's voice moved him to speak up.

"Y-your mother?"

"Yeah, uh, listen, I don't think Dad's up for this just now. It's been a tough day and—"

Morgan could feel Denise's eyes on the back of his head. All he had to do was give her the least encouragement and she'd stay right there, defending his back with figurative sword drawn. Only he couldn't quite care if Delia used him for verbal target practice. He couldn't quite care about anything at the moment. He heard Denise's gulp, felt her emotional withdrawal.

"In that case," she said stiffly, "I'll leave the family to deal with this difficulty. She leaned forward then and pressed a hand to his back. "Call me if you need anything."

Radley nodded for him and tried as best he could to reassure Denise. "It'll be all right. Everyone's just upset right now. I won't let anything get out of hand."

Morgan felt a swelling of pride in his son, and just that single moment of emotion brought a flood of tears to his eyes. He quickly clamped down the emotion, wondering what had happened to the strength he'd felt at Ben's bedside. For one eternal moment, he wavered between explosive emotion and cold numbness. Some inborn sense of self-preservation sent him back over the edge into safe, numb nothing. He didn't even look up as Denise hurried from the room. Neither did he absorb the words swirling around him. They were sounds without meaning, as far as he was concerned, rather like everything else. Suddenly his whole life lacked meaning and he couldn't find the energy to even care.

Chapter Nine

The funeral was simple and dignified and well attended. Radley stood at his father's side, tall and strong, his face showing fierce protectiveness along with his own grief. Delia bawled and wailed and generally painted herself as the only truly loving survivor. Her "dearest friend," Belinda—with her aesthetically thin, hair-transplanted doctor-husband at her side—was a bit more circumspect, but not much. Morgan simply stared straight ahead, his eyes blank, his manner so subdued that it was eerie. He greeted her expressions of concern and sympathy with the same dull mechanics with which he greeted those of everyone else, which was to say, without a flicker of interest. Radley was the one who shook hands and returned hugs, quietly thanking everyone who came to pay their respects, his father blank and silent at his side.

Denise was terribly frightened that the very experience that should have drawn her and Morgan as close as a couple could be was instead driving them apart. Added to that was the loss she felt both of Ben and Jeremy. In many ways it was as if Ben's death had brought back the pain of Jeremy's in all its immediacy, and yet she felt in herself a peaceful kind of acceptance that she had not known previously. She kept seeing again that picture of Ben and Jeremy that Morgan had painted on her mind's eye before his emotional withdrawal.

She kept thinking about that, too, about how everything had changed somehow in the few hours after Morgan and Radley had dropped her at the office and she had returned to them, cashew chicken in tow. She had noticed right away that Morgan had seemed lost and oddly detached, but grief took everyone in a different manner. She had screamed and pleaded for an hour herself and then given way to anger when Jeremy had died. She realized now that she, too, had withdrawn from those who sought only to help and comfort her, but in a much more subtle way than Morgan. She had simply pretended to be well, and carefully arranged her life to put distance between herself and her friends and family, whereas Morgan seemed to have just closed down his emotions entirely. How long before he built the kind of walls around himself that she had, and would she ever be able to scale them, as he had done for her?

The days following the funeral were not encouraging. She carried food to the house, much of it prepared by her own unpracticed hands. Radley received it with thanks and made extravagant compliments concerning its aroma and taste. Morgan looked at her as if she were the newel post that held up a corner of the porch and said nothing.

Radley pushed Morgan to write acknowledgments of all the flowers, plants, cards and gifts of food that found their way into the house. When Denise received hers, she gnashed her teeth in frustration. It read, "Thanks for everything, and tell Chuck thanks, too. Morgan." She could only assume that Chuck had followed through on his offer to send flowers—and Morgan had equated that simple, offhand act with "everything" she had tried to do. It was time to accept the fact that Morgan's love for her—if it had ever actually existed—had died its own quiet death.

So she did the only thing she knew to do; she took refuge in her work and continued privately grieving her losses, just as she had done before Morgan Holt had pushed his way into her life.

Morgan floated up out of sleep, drifting into consciousness. *Drifting* described perfectly all that he did these days. He drifted from one meaningless moment to the next. Sighing, he rolled easily onto his back and opened his eyes to darkness. He was used to waking several times a night now, used to being alone, and he knew from experience that if he just lay quietly and kept his mind a blank, he would drift back off to sleep.

He was almost there, had almost reached oblivion when a distant sound pulled him back. It was that sound that had awakened him, that faraway, almost unrecognizable noise that was clearly out of sync with the night. Radley. His mind immediately provided the solution to an unwanted puzzle. But no, Radley had returned to Fayetteville and college at last. Reiver, then. For some reason, the big dog seemed to resent being shut out of Morgan's bedroom these days. He often whined and scratched at the door. Morgan ignored him, telling himself that he needed sleep and the dog was a distraction.

The sound came again, and he recognized it this time, a kind of rattling knock followed by a startled bark. Morgan resignedly admitted to himself that the sound did not originate with the dog. Burglars, perhaps? He reflected with something akin to amusement that the idea did not alarm him. But then it wasn't very likely. Jasper's weekly police report usually included such heinous crimes as candy stealing and name calling. He supposed that it was someone he knew and that he really ought to get up and see who it was.

Eventually he did so. It was like wading through deep water, but he finally managed to get himself up and into his robe and slippers before walking out onto the landing and down the curving stairs. He noted the blurred silhouette of whomever stood beyond the leaded glass of his front door, backlit by the porch lamp. It definitely had long hair. Denise. He felt a twinge of dread but not enough to make him turn back and pull the covers over his head.

He realized as he drew near that a piece of white paper had been pressed against the glass, and she appeared to be writing on it. Without warning, he opened the door, and she nearly fell into the entry hall on top of him.

"Morgan!"

"Hello."

The dog was there and welcomed her with uncustomary vigor, leaping up and wagging his tail.

"What are you doing walking around in the dark?" she asked Morgan while rubbing the dog's head. "You could've let me know you were there."

"Sorry. Did you want something?"

She pulled back from the dog, folded the envelope on which she had been writing and stuck it into her purse, along with the slender pen she had been using. Reiver sat back on his haunches expectantly. "I, um, wanted to let you know that I'll be out of town a few days."

"Oh."

"I've arranged for my next-door neighbor to feed the cat, but I'd still like it if you kept an eye on the place."

"Sure."

They stood for a moment, each uncertain what to say next, until Morgan realized that he was cold and standing in an open doorway in his bare feet. Obviously, the situation required a remedy. He said the first thing that came to mind. "Well, have a good trip."

That seemed to irritate her for some reason. "Don't you even want to know where I'm going?"

He didn't see really that it mattered, but he politely said, "All right."

She frowned. He felt it, despite the shadows obscuring her face, and that feeling, that sense of her, disturbed him greatly. "I'm going to Chicago on business," she said, and he nodded quickly, desperate to get away.

"I see. Well—"

"Do you?" she said, grasping the door facing. Reiver's tail thumped the floor hopefully once or twice, then subsided. "I don't think you see or hear or feel anything," she added.

He didn't deny it, though at the moment he was feeling a kind of panic he couldn't quite define. She laid her head against the doorjamb, and Reiver stretched out on the floor at his feet, whining with disappointment as it became evident that she wasn't coming in.

"Oh, Morgan, I can't stand this anymore!" she cried. "You said yourself that Ben wanted to be with your mother again. He wanted to go."

"Yes."

"You can't let this beat you! You have to start living again."

"I am."

"No, you're not! You're hung up in denial, and if you don't force yourself out of it we'll never...*you'll* never have a real life again."

She was right, and he knew it, but he couldn't see what she expected him to do about it. He made a feeble attempt to placate her. "We'll have dinner when you get back."

"And discuss what? The weather? The stock market?"

"I don't follow the stock market."

She laughed, but it sounded more like crying. "You made me open up to you. You made me care about you. And now you're essentially telling me that it means nothing to you anymore! Don't you see what's happened? We've traded places, you and I. Now you're the one who can't care about anyone or anything, and I'm the one with her heart broken—again!''

He was disturbed by that. He hadn't meant to break anyone's heart. All he wanted was to be left alone for a time, to get used to the hole in his heart, the emptiness of his life. That wasn't too much to ask, was it? He took a deep breath and repeated the one pacification he'd offered before. ''We'll talk when you get back.''

She gripped the door facing until her fingertips glowed white. ''We won't talk about anything important,'' she said in a whisper aching with sadness. ''We won't talk about anything that matters. Oh, Morgan, I don't want to lose you! I just can't lose anyone I love again!'' With that, she whirled and hurried away.

He watched her pound across the porch and down the steps, then carefully shut the door. Reiver sat up, whining. Morgan ignored him. He had hurt her somehow, and he was sorry about that, but he simply couldn't do anything about it right now. His father, his best friend, his hero, his anchor had left this world and him alone in it. Shouldn't she understand that? He turned from the door and moved sluggishly toward the stairs. Reiver got up and followed, whining still. Morgan thought irritably that he ought to get a cat.

He went to his room and stripped off his robe before lying down on top of the covers. It was cold, and he wanted to cover up, but it seemed like too much effort at the moment. After a bit, he rolled onto his side, curled up his legs, and reached down for whatever covers he could find. He pulled them up all the way to his chin, sighed, and closed his eyes, expecting to drift away. But sleep did not come. He looked at the clock on the dresser and was surprised to find that it was just half past nine. He hadn't been in bed an hour when Denise had awakened him. Suddenly, something that she'd said echoed in his mind, and this time for some reason he really heard it. I just can't lose anyone I love again....

Love. Did Denise love him? Hadn't he wanted that? Why now did the thought bring a kind of panic and the need to flee? Denise was everything he'd ever wanted in a woman. She was bright and confident, stronger, he suspected, than she even knew. She had real style and charm—when she chose to—and her heart was bigger and softer than anyone could expect, considering all she'd been through. He'd told her that Ben had undoubtedly reached out to Jeremy in Heaven in order to comfort her, but ever since, he could only think that he did not want his father there with Jeremy. He wanted him here for himself. In all his life, only his father had stood firmly by him, only his father had ever loved him no matter what, as he was now trying to love Radley.

Radley. Radley had proven himself a capable, compassionate man, the kind of man he tried to be himself. It occurred to him then that, as he loved Radley in the same way that his own father had loved him, then perhaps Radley loved him in the same way that he, Morgan, loved Ben. Did that mean that Radley was looking to him for the same kind of support for which he had looked to Ben? God, how could he ever live up to the legacy of Ben Holt? He thought of the way Belinda nagged at Radley and tried to force her own values on him, how often she expressed disappointment in him, how she undermined his confidence and then criticized him for not being able to choose a profession. What had ever made him think that he could counter that? Had he really believed that he could single-handedly provide the support and wisdom of two parents?

The world seemed a terribly overwhelming place just then, because Ben, his bulwark against the tempests of life, had been removed. For only the second time since he'd sat at the side of his father's deathbed, he cried. He turned his

face to the pillow and let it soak up the tears that rolled
silently from his eyes.

*I just can't lose anyone I love again.... I just can't lose
anyone I love again....*

How had she survived it the first time? he wondered.
Clearly, he hadn't given her enough credit. It had seemed
to him that she was afraid to face the world, to live fully,
to let anyone get close to— The thought ran to a screeching
halt inside his head. God help him, he hadn't been wrong.
She'd reacted just as he had to the death of the most important person in her world, the one who gave her the
strength to do what life requires. Just like him. Except that
he had Radley. Suddenly he was so very grateful for his
son and for Denise and for what he'd had with his parents,
for a wise and wonderful father and a kind, loving mother.
His quiet tears turned into sobs that were a mixture of
laughter and pain.

It was cold, not as cold as Chicago, but cold enough to
have her shivering inside her warm-up suit. She ran from
the parking lot, a gust of wind slamming the heavy metal
door behind her as she entered the club building. Several
heads turned. Some people recognized her and called out
hellos or acknowledged her with waves. She felt a surprising satisfaction in so many friendly greetings. They seemed
to say that she was home. Jasper was really home for her
now. She hadn't felt that she had a place in this world in
so long that she hardly knew how to respond. She smiled,
stiffly at first and then warmly, and gave back little waves
of her own.

After checking in, she went to the posting board to see
what activities were available. An aerobics class was about
to begin, also a coed basketball game. Water isometrics
classes were conducted every hour on the half hour through
eight o'clock. She hadn't brought a swimsuit, and the other
activities didn't particularly appeal to her. She supposed

she could go for a run around the rubber track and finish off with a half hour in the weight room, but running had never been her favorite sport. She stepped over and checked out the racquetball court reservation sheet, finding an open slot in about forty minutes. She penciled in her name and attached a red sticker beside it, indicating that she needed a partner. That done, she wandered over to a crowd gathered to watch the half-court basketball game that the volunteer ref had just whistled to a start. She'd spend fifteen or twenty minutes mingling, and if she hadn't found a partner by then, she'd release the court and take that run, after all.

She was about to do just that when she glanced toward the outside door and saw Morgan walk past the check-in station wearing street clothes, the pockets of his corduroy coat bulging suspiciously. He gave the studly male attendant a smile and a slight wave, spoke briefly and wandered into the busy gymnasium, turning his head this way and that as if searching for someone. Denise bowed her head and bit her lip. Was he looking for someone specific? A friend? A date? All she knew for sure was that he wasn't looking for her. As far as he knew, she was still in Illinois. On the edge of the crowd, she turned away, but then she stopped.

Morgan had been distressingly persistent about getting to know her. It was because of him, really, that she had let down the barriers and allowed herself to start fitting in here. He was the reason this place had become home to her. What if he had been as easily discouraged as she was feeling now? She might still be getting her only welcomes, however tentative, from that snotty cat of hers. On the other hand, if he rebuffed her again... Well, she wasn't sure that it would be wise to solicit such an experience in public. She stood uncertainly for several moments, debating her options, only to let someone else beat her to the draw.

"Hey, Morgan!" She whirled around in time to catch a glimpse of one of her neighbors as he pushed past her, moving in Morgan's direction. Morgan stopped and waited for the young man to reach him. They shook hands. The man clapped him on the shoulder, speaking deliberately. Morgan nodded and managed a wan smile, then nodded again. Denise knew exactly what was being said. Glad to see you out and about. Sorry about your loved one. Let me know if there's anything I can do. I know what you're going through because my grandmother-aunt-cousin-stepsister passed away six, seven, eight years ago. And so on and so forth, all of it very nearly meaningless because no one can know just what another person feels or thinks...unless the bond of love and shared experience is so strong that it transcends the normal barriers of skin and bone. But she knew. Oh, yes, she did. She knew exactly what he'd been through, exactly. Which was why she should be there beside him now. Putting aside her fear of rejection, she crossed the room toward him, getting there just as her neighbor clapped him once more on the upper arm and left him.

He hadn't seen her yet. His eyes were closed and his head bowed as he took a deep, fortifying breath.

"Hi."

His head snapped up, eyes gone wide. "Denise! I didn't know you were back."

"I just got in a little while ago."

"And your first thought was to come here?"

She shrugged. "I was feeling kind of restless."

He nodded and ran a hand over his head. "I know what you mean."

"Do you? That's a good sign."

"Is it? I don't know." He shook his head and added softly, "It's so much more difficult than I expected."

She reached out a hand to him, laying it tentatively upon his forearm. "I know."

He covered her hand with his. "I know you do."

They stood that way for a moment, and then he abruptly pulled back. "Listen, I, uh, could use a sponsor. I told the attendant that I was just looking for someone when I came in. I figure that he's ready to throw me out right about now."

She smiled. "No problem—providing you're willing to give me a game of racquetball. I have a court reserved for twenty minutes from now."

"Great. Uh, I can't promise you a top-level game, though."

"That's all right. I don't have anything to prove, just working off some excess energy and whiling away some time."

"Okay. Sounds good."

"Just let me clear this with the gatekeeper," she said, moving off in that direction. In only a matter of seconds she had Morgan's name on the guest list, hers beside it in the sponsor column. She walked back to him, and together they made their way to the back of the building.

In the communal area outside the courts and the showers, Morgan stripped off his street clothes, revealing skin-hugging silks beneath. Quickly he slipped on a pair of loose shorts and sat down next to Denise on the bench to pull on his socks and court shoes while she did likewise. She finished first and began stretching. He joined her shortly, and they worked in a silence that was only slightly uncomfortable. Time passed quickly, and the court emptied right on schedule. Denise removed her warm-up suit and took a final few stretches before getting out her racquet and balls.

Morgan followed her into the room, wheeling his arm to loosen the joints. Denise took the first serve without preamble. His return was sluggish, as well as the next and the next, but she cut him no slack. Instead she drove him, on and on, right to the very edge of his endurance and ability. When it was over, he was breathing much too hard, and she was much too energetic still.

"Again," he said tersely, disgusted that he had allowed himself to deteriorate to such a state. How many weeks had it been since he'd had a real workout? He didn't care to count them.

"You sure?" she asked, sounding slightly more breathless than he'd expected.

He merely nodded and served the ball. She went after him with every ounce of her strength—and beat him down to his knees, literally. Exhausted, he missed the shot and dropped, huffing through his mouth. She pattered over to the ball and bent to scoop it up, then came back to stand over him.

"You okay?"

"Yeah." It took him a while to get the one word out.

She glanced at the clock on the wall. "We've run over about two minutes."

He nodded and lifted a hand for assistance. She bent and slipped a hand beneath his arms, helping him up. He reeled slightly, then found his feet. "Thanks."

She stepped away, and he was grateful. It was embarrassing enough without her thinking she would have to help him from the room. His strength returned in time to get him out the door and across to the bench.

Denise went through her cool-down routine without so much as a glance in his direction, then tugged on her warm-up suit and changed her shoes. He'd managed to get down to his bare feet by then and take out his fresh clothing.

"I planned to shower at home," she said, then amended herself. "Actually, I'm thinking of a long, hot soak in the tub, so I guess I'll take off now."

Her words conjured a sensually vivid image for him—candles surrounding a steaming tub, Denise with her hair pinned up, wet skin gleaming. Impulsively he followed up on her statement as best he could, given the situation.

"I think I'd better shower here, but if you'll wait I'll be quick."

She seemed surprised—and a little wary. "Oh, I don't know..."

"Seems to me I promised you a talk," he prodded, adding, "Come on. After beating my socks off, it's the least you can do."

One corner of her mouth quirked up in a half smile. "Okay, but..." She glanced around them at the throng of milling people.

She was right. No place to talk here. "Never mind. I'll meet you back at the apartment in a few minutes, okay?"

She shrugged. "Yeah, okay. Just give me time for a quick shower."

He grinned. "Sorry about that bath."

She flipped a hand. "I can take a bath anytime."

He wanted to tell her that they could take a bath together later, but the words seemed impertinent at best. She wasn't exactly showering him with affection at the moment, not that he blamed her, and the confusing feeling that it wasn't the right time for them nagged at him. "Half an hour," he said, and she nodded before turning and walking away.

He rushed through a hot shower and quickly dressed, rushing out with damp hair. The wind nearly sliced his ears off, it was so cold. He knew that he'd better hurry home and get out the hair dryer before he did anything else. Once there, combing through hair that badly needed a trim, he found himself not wanting to go out again at all. Determinedly, he pushed that inclination aside, bundled himself into a coat, knit cap and gloves and hurried across the yard to Denise's door.

She was wearing fluffy house shoes, white knit leggings, and the big comfy sweater that she'd worn the first time he'd taken her to meet his father. She had a towel wrapped around her head and a hard brush with widely spaced bristles in one hand. He stepped up inside and pulled the door closed behind him, shutting out the cold bite of the wind.

"Take off your coat and come into the living room where it's warm," she said. "I hope you don't mind, I have to brush out my hair."

"Of course I don't mind." He took off his coat and hung it on the doorknob to the coat closet, stuffing cap and gloves into the pockets, before following her into the living room. She curled up on the armchair positioned beside the window, and he took the seat opposite her on the couch. Her cat hopped up into her lap and stretched out over the length of her thighs much as if she were a conveniently shaped pillow. "I don't think that cat appreciates you," Morgan said with a touch of humor.

She wrinkled her nose. "This cat doesn't appreciate anything. Frankly, I'm beginning to think I ought to get a dog." She said it pointedly at Smithson, but then she scratched between his ears. The animal closed his eyes and indulged himself in a nap. Denise reached up and unwound the towel from her head. Her dark hair tumbled in shiny strands around her head and shoulders. She put the brush to her scalp and began tearing through.

"What are you doing?" Morgan blurted, appalled.

"Brushing the tangles out of my hair."

"You're going to yank yourself bald!"

She grimaced. "Don't worry. I'm used to it. When your hair is this thick and long, you don't have much choice." She attacked it again, yanking the hard brush through it mercilessly. "Actually," she said through her teeth, "I've been thinking about cutting it."

He couldn't sit still for that. "Don't you dare!" He was on his feet and moving toward her before he thought about what he intended. Reaching out for the brush, he decided not to think about it. "Give me that."

Surprised, she handed it over more meekly than he'd

have thought possible. He walked around behind her and began gently working through the wet tangles when she sat forward. He worked for some time, thoroughly enjoying himself. It had a life of its own, this hair. He'd fantasized about this hair, and by golly he wouldn't see it disappear, not when he could help her with it. "Cut your hair?" he said dismissively. "I like this hair." He brushed through another long strand and laid it aside to take up one more. "In fact, I love this hair. I don't want you to cut it." He worked through the rest, laid aside the brush, and gathered its weight into his hands, feeling the heaviness of it, the vibrancy, the richness. "Don't cut it. Please."

He heard her swallow and recognized the tremor in her voice when she said, "All right. I promise."

He walked around the chair and reached down for her, pulling her up and into his arms. She came easily, readily, willingly, her own arms sliding around his waist. Against the curve of his neck she whispered, "I've missed you."

He tilted her face up and cupped it with his hands. Gazing down into her eyes, he saw his own hurt and fears reflected there. "Teach me how to get through this," he said softly. "Give me the time to work through it."

"Yes," she said, and her gaze narrowed to his mouth. He laid it gently against her own, his eyelids drifting closed, and he thought, I want to marry this woman. But hard on the heels of that surprising realization came another: his father would never see him married and happy, though it had been his fondest wish to do so. A sadness so sharp that it cut pierced him. He felt an almost irrational need to bury that sadness beneath the sensuous touch of this woman, but he recognized it as the same blind need for oblivion that had kept him beneath the covers of his bed too many mornings of late, and he wouldn't let loving Denise be that. When he made love to her, it would be in celebration and commitment, not in pain. He turned his face away, saying, "I'm sorry."

"Why?"

He shook his head. "This grief, it attacks you in every vulnerable moment. I know I felt it when Mother died, but I held it at bay with the comforting knowledge that I still had Pop. I heaped my need of her on him, and now it feels doubly hard to lose him."

"I know. I know. I sublimated my grief over the end of my marriage in my joy of my son. I had everything invested in him, and when he died…"

He hugged her close. "I'm so sorry. What a callous fool you must have thought me, trying to push you past the loss."

"No. You were right, Morgan. The living have to go on. I knew it, but I didn't want to. You made me face it. Ben made me face it."

"Ben?"

She nodded. "Because he was ready to die, Morgan. He was ready. It's a marvelous gift, that, being ready when the time comes, because it has to come for all of us. But it hasn't come for me—or for you—and it's not going to for a long time. I want to be ready when it does, and I think the only way to do that must be to live a life of love, a life so full that it just can't encompass another moment. My son didn't have that, and I felt for a long time that because he didn't, I mustn't. But I was wrong. That's what Ben taught me. That's what he was trying to tell me when he sent you out of the cabin and told me bluntly how well you can love."

He felt himself tremble at that, felt a coldness settle over his heart. Tears started in his eyes. He said in a broken voice, "I'm not sure that's still true."

"Yes it is," she told him flatly. "It has to be. Because I need you, Morgan. I need you so much."

The ice melted, leaving him aching and vulnerable but willing, at least. "I'll try," he whispered. "For you I'll try."

She hugged him close for a long, warm moment, but then she pulled back and squared her shoulders. He'd seen that look before, and he didn't much want to know what was behind it now, but did he really have a choice? "You can start with Christmas," she announced.

He recoiled from the very thought. Christmas. Snow covering his father's fresh grave. That sadness stabbed him again. "I don't think I can, not this year."

"Oh, yes," she said, as firm as any military officer he'd ever known. "It won't be fun. It'll feel like a travesty, in fact, but the next one will be easier and the next and the next. The thing is not to put it off. Don't let next year be the first. Let it be easier. Remember that we need you, Radley and I. We need you to live and to be happy again and to love us."

He knew with a certain shame that he'd rather have crawled back into his lair just then, but Ben wouldn't have wanted that. Ben had prepared him for this as best he could, and now it was up to him. And there was Radley to think of. If the world retained any shred of order, then one day Radley would have to survive the death of his own father. Perhaps he and Denise together... But he was getting ahead of himself. Christmas had to be gotten through. He took a deep breath and nodded his head.

"All right, sweetheart," he said. "Show me how to do Christmas."

Chapter Ten

Denise and Radley really got into decorating the house, even though Morgan remained, at best, a casual observer. When she called up Radley and proposed that they help his father celebrate the holidays, he pledged himself to whatever she had in mind, and that sort of started the ball rolling. She began to envision a real Victorian Christmas, complete with a real Christmas tree and real pine boughs and real candles and real goodies baked up in the kitchen. Radley himself came up with the idea for a real Yule log. The obvious place to go out and cut down their very own tree and boughs was the homestead up on the mountain, but neither Denise nor Radley wanted to expose Morgan to that just yet, so Radley got permission from a professor at school to cut on his land up around Pea Ridge.

It had snowed the day before they set out to get the tree and again that very morning, laying down a clean, silent, white blanket that got deeper and deeper the higher the elevation. Pea Ridge wasn't all that high, so they decided to bundle up and go on out after the tree. Morgan good-naturedly agreed to go along and drive the truck, but when they found what Denise proclaimed to be the perfect tree, Radley announced that he'd cut it down all by himself, and Morgan, uncharacteristically, let him. Afterward, all three tramped off in search of perfect boughs, taking one here and another there so that no tree stood denuded. It took, literally, hours, but Denise had meant to make a day of it all along. She'd packed a picnic lunch, complete with baked potatoes, a thermos of hot cocoa, and a cherry cobbler still steaming when she'd wrapped it.

She picked a sunny spot next to a stone wall and made the guys clear away the snow in a ten-foot circle before putting down a heavy layer of rugs and unpacking the hamper. They ate like lumberjacks, especially Radley, who'd done all the heavy work. His energy recouped, he then eyed the ring of churned snow that bordered their picnic spot. Denise recognized the glint of little-boy mischief in his eyes but not quickly enough to keep from being pelted.

All-out snow war ensued. Morgan got up and ran far enough away to keep out of the line of fire, but before they were done, he was doubled over with laughter, and that made it all worth it, even the hit to the face that shoved snow up her nose and made her teeth scream with cold. It was great fun, the kind of fun that she had denied herself for so long in order to hold on to a selfish, self-defeating grief, the kind of fun she never wanted Morgan to miss out on, even though he couldn't join in wholeheartedly just then.

They spent the remainder of the day and evening decorating the tree and weaving garlands. Radley put the Yule log into a brandy-and-spice bath to soak, per the instructions of his college professor, and filled the house with the exotic scent of Christmas. Over the next few days, Denise strung cranberries until her fingertips were bright red, stacked apples and cinnamon sticks in artful arrangements, did the same with oranges and mint leaves, and scoured the attics for usable decorations. She bought a truckload of

ribbons and lace, fancy filigreed ornaments and slender
candles. When she'd dressed the house in its Victorian holiday best, with Radley as her willing assistant, she then
took over Morgan's kitchen and threw herself into baking
with wild abandon.

Morgan was interested enough to nibble whenever he
got the chance, and once she even pressed him into joining
Radley at the table to decorate gingerbread men, only to
come up with very un-Victorian-like football and hockey
players in numbered jerseys and helmets. They laughed
when she scolded them, and then she laughed, too, because
they really were very cute gingerbread football and hockey
players. Afterward, when Radley had left for the long drive
back to Fayetteville, Morgan pulled her down into his lap
and kissed the tip of her nose, saying that for a while there
they had seemed like a real family, the three of them, and
she was amazed by how very desperately she coveted the
notion.

The real surprise came a few days later when she proposed a dinner party. Radley, for one, was very much in
favor of the idea, admitting shyly that he had been meaning
for some time to introduce his father to a certain young
woman of his acquaintance. Without that added induce-
ment, Morgan more than likely would have balked at the
idea, but he clearly couldn't resist the lure of meeting Radley's young woman. He did ask her, very seriously, to keep
it small. She decided to put the leaf in his dining table and
seat ten. After much discussion the guest list evolved to
include an old friend of Morgan's named Lincoln Carlton
and his wife Mavis, as well as Denise's secretary Betty
and her husband Cleeve and, another surprise, Jess and
Helen Faber, parents of Radley's as yet unmet Leanne,
both of whom Radley seemed to know well enough to
guarantee their acceptance of the invitation.

That evening, after Radley again insisted on driving
back to Fayetteville, the reason for which being no longer

unclear, Morgan couldn't help speculating about the relationship between his son and the mysterious Leanne.

"This is sounding pretty serious all of a sudden. Wonder how long he's known her?"

"Long enough to get to know her parents, apparently," Denise said.

"Why hasn't he said anything about her before?"

Disliking the tone of worry in his voice, she sought to reassure him by stating the obvious. "Radley said he'd been meaning to introduce her for some time now."

Morgan waved that away with a jerk of his hand. "You know young people. That could mean for the past week."

"Or month, or even six months."

He shook his head. "Why haven't I heard about her before now then?"

"Maybe the time was just never right, Morgan. I mean, you have been preoccupied of late. Maybe he was afraid to worry you."

"I'm not the worrying sort."

"Not until recently," she said gently.

He was rocked back by that. She saw a flare of anger in his eyes, but then it faded, and she watched him mull over the implications of what she'd said. After some minutes, he sighed and nodded. "Is that normal?" he asked. "I mean, after a loss, it seems to me it would be normal to start to worry about the surviving loved ones."

She smiled sadly at that. "I think it must be. I remember that after Jeremy died I was almost obsessed with the idea that my mother would be killed in a car accident. She was never the best of drivers. In fact, if her errands took her farther than the immediate neighborhood, she used to call me or my sister to drive her around. But we used to laugh and joke about it, you know? Then suddenly it took on a much more ominous feeling."

"I feel like a traitor suddenly," Morgan admitted. "I'm the one who's been telling everyone to get off Rad's back and let him make his own decisions. Then he more or less announces that he has a girl, and I'm worried he's picked a nag like his mother and will spend the rest of his life regretting it.'' He winced and added, ''Yikes, I can't believe I said that.''

''What, that Belinda's a nag or that Radley isn't smart enough to go for a different sort?''

''Both.''

Denise got up from her seat on the couch and walked over to him where he stood, leaning against the fireplace mantel. ''You're only human, after all, my darling.''

He smiled at that. ''Am I?''

''Afraid so.''

''Your darling, I mean.''

She slid her arms about his waist. ''More and more every day.''

He wrapped his arms around her, holding her close. After a moment he said, ''I'm sorry I haven't been more enthusiastic about things.''

''You've been fine,'' she told him firmly, ''and I know it hasn't been easy.''

''I keep thinking how much Pop would enjoy everything if he were here.''

''I know.''

''Was it like that for you?''

''It still is,'' she said. ''The difference this year is that I have someone else to care about, someone to make it better for.''

He clamped his hand in her hair at the nape of her neck and tugged her head back so that he could look down into her face. ''Have I told you yet that I love you?''

Her heart leaped to hyperspeed, but she very deliberately shook her head. ''No, and I'm not sure that I want you to yet.''

He cocked his head. ''Why is that?''

She made herself be very cool and very logical about

this. "You've suffered—and are still suffering—a very great loss. You can't know with absolute certainty what you're feeling just now, and this is too important to take a chance of misreading those feelings. I'm not going anywhere anytime soon. I can wait until the time is right—for both of us."

"Mmm, there goes that feeling again, the one you're not sure I'm sure about."

She laughed. "I hope so. I really do."

He dipped his head and kissed her firmly on the mouth. Within moments it became a scalding exercise in frustration, wherein skin tried unabashedly to meet skin despite the barrier of clothing, and tongues tried to plumb new depths beyond the mating dance created for them. Hands tried to touch souls. Lips went for permanent bonds. The desire of the body clearly meant to ignore the sensible safeguards laid down by the mind. Morgan was the first to find the strength to push back.

"You'd better get out of here," he said raggedly, "before whether or not we know what we're doing becomes a moot point."

She left with a smile on her face.

It was one little irritation after another for Morgan. She wanted him to wear a tie for a dinner served in his own home, and even though he knew that normally it wouldn't matter a fig, tonight it seemed just too much to ask. He reminded himself that she was trying her little heart out. She wanted him to have a happy holiday. He put on the tie.

But then she wanted him to banish Reiver to the cold, snowy out-of-doors, and it really was just too much. He said something unplanned and really stupid about Reiver being his best friend and how she'd behaved the one and only time that wicked cat of hers had been out in the great outdoors. She said nothing about the stupid cat being declawed or blaming him for the cat getting out of its carrier when he was standing ten yards away. Instead, she kissed him on the cheek and capitulated sweetly, saying, "You're absolutely right, Morg. I forget how much better behaved Reiver is than Smithson. It's just, well, he's a little smelly."

Actually, "a little smelly" was an understatement. Morgan took his tie off and gave Reiver a quick bath in the shower. He'd been meaning to do it for a couple of days anyway. He'd been meaning to do several things for a couple of days, most of which he caught Denise or Radley doing at some point, like laying a fire on the hearth and dusting the chandelier over the dining table. He was being a beast, and he knew it. Yet, when the first party-goers arrived at the door and Denise called out from the kitchen that he should get it, he felt a spurt of resentment.

After that, he was too busy playing host to feel much of anything. He didn't even have time, really, to form much of a first impression of Radley's Leanne. Her parents were another matter. The Fabers were a walking contradiction. Jess, Mr. Faber, was a small, balding, meek sort who seemed constantly pained by one thing or another, while Helen, Mrs. Faber, stood nearly six feet tall and spoke with a voice like a cannon boom. Morgan found himself hoping inanely that Leanne was adopted.

Denise's secretary, Betty, and her husband, Cleeve, arrived before he had time to make more than the most cursory conversation with the Fabers. Betty was a grandmotherly type, and dressed, Morgan guessed, much as she would be for a day at the office. Cleeve was a retired professor of economics and looked every inch the part from his balding pate to the patches on the elbows of his gray tweed jacket and the jaunty bow tie dressing his Adam's apple, red in deference to the holiday season, apparently. Both were clearly uncertain and yet not intimidated. Almost with relief, Morgan realized that he liked them, especially when Betty took one of his hands in hers and said quietly how very sorry she was about his father's passing.

"And I can tell you," she confided in a near whisper, "it shook our Ms. Jenkins as nothing else I've ever seen has done. But then I didn't know about her little son before. She never mentioned it until after your father, you see." She smiled suddenly and added more firmly, "I'm so glad that you have each other now."

Morgan found himself smiling in return. "So am I."

Linc and Mavis arrived then. True to form, Linc pounded on the door and then merely opened it and walked in. Mavis swept in behind him, slipped her coat from her shoulders and dropped it over Linc's arm in one smooth movement, her head pivoting at the end of her neck as she took in everything around her. "The house is marvelous!" she exclaimed, gliding toward him with that ever-present homecoming-queen grin in place.

Linc hung the coat on the hall tree and followed at the more sedate pace required by the lack of movement in his right knee. A hideous break during a football game their junior year at the University of Arkansas had put an end to his dreams of playing pro ball and sent him into banking instead. Neither his attitude nor his wallet had suffered. In his usual straightforward manner, he wasted no breath on small talk, saying instead, "Been worried about you! Damned glad to get the invitation. I suppose we have that beauty who was mooning over you at the funeral to thank. Where is she then?"

Morgan chuckled. "In the kitchen, thank you."

Linc's dignified silver brows rose in tandem. "Domesticated her, have you? Damn, there's hope for you yet."

"That's the next vice president of Wholesale International you're talking about, and if you offend her she's liable to snatch that tongue right out of your head."

"Yeow! I like her already."

"You'd better."

"Get me a drink, host, and remember it's the season for generosity."

"Come on then."

He took Linc into the parlor, made introductions all around and manned the bar until everyone was settled, then he excused himself to check on Denise, leaving Radley in charge. He found her scrutinizing a cookbook, wire whisk in hand and muttering to herself. "Need a hand?"

She started at the sound of his voice and whirled around. Her apron had been scorched, and she had flour on her chin. "Morgan! Thank God! I'm afraid I've ruined the sauce! It got so thick so quickly! I took it off the fire, but it's all curdled looking, so I thought I'd better start over, but first I—" The buzzer went off on the oven. "Oh! The roast!" She literally tossed the whisk at the counter and ran to the oven. Yanking open the door she reached inside with her bare hands.

"Denise!" Morgan snatched pot holders off the counter and shoved her out of the way. "Are you nuts? You'll burn your hands!"

He brought the roasting pan out. Denise took one look and wailed, "Oh, no! I've burned it!"

"It's not ruined," he told her, "just a little overdone. We can fix it."

"How?"

"I need a tin of pâté from the pantry, a bottle of sherry, Worcestershire, mustard and that syringe with the huge needle in the left-hand drawer there by the refrigerator." While she went to gather those things, he took a knife and trimmed off the worst of the black. It wasn't too bad, really, but it wasn't very elegant, either. Well, they'd fix that. Working quickly, he injected the roast liberally with a mixture of sherry and Worcestershire. Next he blended the pâté and mustard and spread it over the roast, coating it evenly. Finally, he used the knife to quickly create a crosshatch pattern in the coating. "There. We'll let it set a few minutes while I make the sauce and you get changed. Everyone's here, you know. I have Rad playing host.''

Denise gasped and yanked at her apron. ''Why didn't you tell me?''

''I thought you knew. We haven't exactly been tiptoeing around in there.''

''Where did you put my things?''

''In the room next to mine.''

''Damn! I've ruined everything!''

Chuckling, he wiped his hands on a dish towel and pulled her to him, kissing her quickly on the mouth. ''You haven't ruined anything. Now get moving.''

She started away, then turned back and said, ''Put in the bread, will you? fifteen minutes at 350.''

''Will do.''

She kissed him hard on the mouth and literally ran for the back stairs. Laughing, he shook his head and got down to business.

Somehow—he'd never quite understand it—she beat him back to the parlor. He heard her laughter as he crossed the entry hall and stopped in the doorway to see for himself if she really was already there. She was definitely there. And the sight of her fairly knocked his eyeballs out. She had piled her hair up loosely on top of her head and clipped a pair of dime-sized rhinestones to her earlobes, and she wore a dress that made his mouth water. It was as red as her lipstick and long-sleeved and fitted and short, with a neckline that came all the way up to her collarbone in front and plunged to her waist in back. She had little red shoes on her feet with closed toes supporting huge rhinestones and no backs whatsoever, and unless he missed his guess, she wasn't wearing any stockings—or much of anything else beneath that dress. He'd seen bikinis that weren't as sexy as that getup, and suddenly it was all he could do to shut his mouth and swallow.

"Ah, our host!" Lincoln said. "Thought you'd abandoned us."

"I—" Morgan cleared his throat and moved into the room. "I got waylaid in the kitchen."

"Thank God one of us can really cook!" Denise said. "Otherwise, I'm afraid we'd be calling out for pizza!"

Everyone laughed but Morgan. He walked across the room and slid his arm around her waist in a blatant gesture of possession. "She's being too modest," he said, more for her ears than anyone else's. "I made the sauce while she made herself beautiful. Now which one of us knows best what she's doing?"

She literally blushed, but she smiled, too, and it occurred to him that he was feeling mighty good just now. He got them both drinks and steered her toward the fainting couch. Everyone was talking and laughing when the buzzer went off in the kitchen. He set it a couple minutes early to allow for time getting to it. "That's the bread," he said, starting to rise.

"No, let me," Denise said, handing him her glass. "We'll do this family-style if no one objects," she said over her shoulder as she moved toward the door. "I'll have it on the table in a jiffy."

"I'm all for serving myself," Lincoln said. "Everyone else seems to underestimate my appetite."

"Honestly, Morg, you'd think I starved him!" Mavis complained cheerfully.

"No one who can see him thinks you starve him, Mavis," Rad quipped.

After the laughter died down, Helen Faber said, "Looking at him, you'd think I starved Jess, but the man eats his weight three times a day, I swear, while I get fat on lettuce and carrots."

"You're not fat, Helen," Jess Faber said softly. "You're big, and there's a difference."

"Radley's the real eater," Leanne said then, her voice silky and cultured, "but it never shows."

"It will," Morgan promised. "Wait'll he hits forty."

"Or fifty!" Betty and Cleeve chimed.

The conversation went on in that vein until Denise slid open the door to the formal dining room and announced that dinner was on the table. It was a fine dinner made excellent by the company. Afterward they sat around the parlor listening to recorded Christmas music and chatting amongst themselves. At one point Mavis stole Denise away, and the two of them conversed gaily for several long minutes, during which Morgan looked on indulgently, as pleased and at peace as he'd ever been. Somehow he had crossed a threshold tonight. His eyes went to Denise, and he thought to himself that she had meant for him to make a transition tonight. She had pushed him back into life, and he was suddenly so very grateful that he felt on the verge of tears. Reiver padded up next to his chair then and lay down at his feet, snuffling a deep sigh of contentment. It was a sentiment Morgan both understood and shared. Life was good. Life was very good.

Christmas day began cold and gray. Without fresh snowfall, the fields and yards had grown muddy and dirty. But Denise's mood would not be dampened. She thought of the smiles Morgan wore more often these past days and of the long kisses and secret looks they shared daily. The anticipation of what must surely come was utterly delicious, but wearing at times, so much so that she literally fled back to the haven of her own apartment in the late evenings. But one day, she told herself, one day that would not be necessary.

She hopped out of bed and ground beans for coffee, letting it brew while she showered and dressed in red stirrup pants and a matching sweater embroidered with green and gold. She swept her hair back with a wide red band

and clipped small gold hoops to her earlobes. While she sipped her coffee, she took out the presents that she had purchased for Morgan and took great pleasure in wrapping them in dark green paper printed with small red squares lined with gold. She attached a huge gold bow to the package containing the new racquet and case, a red one to the driving gloves and a green one to the engraved key chain and matching money clip. Radley's gifts had been wrapped some days ago, but she'd saved Morgan's for today, occasionally taking them out and looking at them in the interim. They weren't anything special, but she had chosen them with love and care, taking great pleasure in doing so.

As she filled Smithson's bowl, the telephone rang.

"Hello."

It was Morgan. "What's keeping you? Breakfast is ready." He sounded hungry and happy.

She laughed. "I'm on my way." She shoved the gifts into a bright red paper bag, stomped her feet into white snow boots and slung on a white parka with a rabbit-lined hood.

Morgan opened the door before she got to it and came out to meet her on the porch. He threw his arms around her. "Merry Christmas! Wow, look at the loot!"

They hurried into the house together. Radley was pouring orange juice and champagne in the dining room. Morgan had laid on the promised feast, providing everything from pecan waffles to eggs and hash browns, ham, bacon and sausage. There were biscuits as big as her fist, strawberries and pineapple and banana, maple and blueberry syrup, Irish oatmeal fragrant with cinnamon and brown sugar, and croissants drizzled with honey. "We can't eat all this!" Denise exclaimed.

"Speak for yourself," Rad told her, grabbing a plate.

They actually made quite a dent before adjourning to the parlor to divvy up the gifts. Denise was surprised at the haul she made, until she saw that her family had sent her

gifts in care of Morgan. It was great fun. They took turns
ripping open the packages, exclaiming over every gift like
children. Radley's gift to her was a beautifully framed
photo of his father. Morgan's was breathtaking, a narrow
gold choker with what looked suspiciously like a diamond
drop that could be easily transferred to a longer chain or a
brooch. With it was a miniature version that she first took
for a bracelet. A closer look showed that a name had been
engraved inside, the name of her cat!

"That one's a fake," he said, pointing at the "diamond"
drop on the cat's collar, "but don't tell him. He'll never
forgive me."

She threw her arms around him. "You shouldn't have!"

"Oh, I'm not finished," he promised her. "Get your
coat. Rad will make the place presentable and keep brunch
warm for the Fabers."

"They're coming?"

"They're taking us out to dinner later," Radley informed her. Shaking a finger at his father he said, "Don't
forget."

Morgan grinned. "Cross my heart."

Rad kissed Denise on the cheek and thanked her for the
sweater and wallet. She noted a secretive twinkle in his
blue eyes.

Morgan made a point of tugging on his driving gloves
as they walked out to the truck.

"Where are we going?"

He shook his head. "No questions. You'll see."

When they turned back into the foothills above Fayetteville, she knew, but she wisely said nothing. Clearly he
had a plan, and whatever else was afoot, he was ready for
a return to the cabin. She hoped that she was, too, but she
need not have worried. It was rather like going home, pulling up in that sloping yard. The snow was still deep and
pristine here, except where someone had already been.
Smoke wafted from the chimney, and the wonderful aroma

of steaming apple cider reached her the instant she opened her door. Morgan took her hand and together they climbed up onto the porch, but instead of going inside, Morgan led her to the end of the porch looking out over the valley below. The sun had come out and a billowy white cloud floated upon the horizon above Fayetteville in the distance. The silence was absolute, the peace palpable.

Denise squeezed his hand. "It's so beautiful here."

He took a deep breath and blew it out again, frosting the air. "Yes. Yes, it is. That's one reason I wanted to be here for this."

She wanted to ask him what "this" was, but something told her to let him come at it in his own way. He pulled her in front of him and wrapped his arms around her shoulders, holding her against his chest.

"This thing with Rad and Leanne is looking pretty serious."

"Yes, it is. How do you feel about that?"

He shrugged. "Well, she's not what I expected him to choose, but I can't say I'm disappointed. She obviously adores him, and the Fabers certainly seem to approve. They've asked him to come into their business after he graduates next year."

"Have they? What business is that?"

"Faber's Furniture."

"Oh, my goodness! I never even put it together!"

"I wondered, but I didn't want to ask. Jess Faber made the offer last night. I rather expect an announcement at dinner tonight."

"An engagement, you mean?"

He nodded. "That's my guess."

She bit her lip. It was none of her business, but she couldn't help saying it. "He's awfully young."

"Yes, he is. Leanne is actually a couple years older than him. I'm afraid I'll have to insist on a long engagement, at least until he graduates."

"Think he'll fight you?"

"Actually, I don't. Faber gave me the feeling that Leanne herself needs at least a year to finish her master's in early childhood education. According to him, he'd hoped she'd come into the business, but she has her heart set on teaching kindergarten."

"So how are you feeling about all this?" she asked, turning within the circle of his arms.

He smiled down at her. "Slow off the mark."

"What do you mean?"

"I mean, I'm not going to practice what I preach, at least not what I intend to preach to my son."

"Which is?"

"Patience."

She shook her head. "I'm not following you."

He merely smiled and stroked his thumb over her bottom lip, the leather of his glove as soft as satin. "I wish Ben were here," he said softly.

She locked her arms about his waist. "I know. So do I."

"But maybe it's better that he's not, for what I have in mind."

She could only cock her head and admit, "Morgan, you're confusing me."

His eyes roamed over her face, that oddly poignant smile still in place. Finally, he switched his gaze back to the valley below, saying, "I have a favor to ask, a large one."

"All right. What is it?"

"I want to spend my wedding night here."

Denise reeled inwardly. "W-wedding night?"

"Wedding night," he confirmed. "I want to spend it here, and I want to do it soon."

He'd taken her by such surprise that her mouth was hanging open. He closed it gently with a hand beneath her chin and then kissed it tenderly.

"I love you, Denise, and I've never been more certain

of anything. I think that you love me, too, almost as much as I love you.''

"More!" she exclaimed. "Oh, I love you so much!"

He beamed down at her. "So. Will you marry me…soon?"

Her mouth was hanging open again, but she couldn't have gotten a word out of it anyway. All she could do was nod her head and throw her arms around his neck, going up on tiptoe to hug him tightly enough to cut off his breath. Laughing, he pried her off and kissed her hotly, saying afterward, "I'll take that as a yes."

She laughed, tears spilling from her eyes.

"None of that now," he said softly, tugging off one glove to thumb away the droplets. "We've cried enough for several lifetimes, the two of us, and really, darling, we have so much to be happy about. We've suffered losses, yes, but only because we had so much to lose. It occurred to me the other day, you know, that my sister will never know the depth of grief that I have because she's never known the kind of love that I have. It was there for her, but somehow she couldn't accept it. I wonder how many of us can? The thing is, though, not to get trapped by the pain. You showed me that."

"Only because you showed me first," she said, sniffing.

He laughed, not because she'd said anything humorous but from sheer joy. "Your parents will come for the wedding, won't they, and Troy and May and the kids?"

"I'm sure they will."

He slipped an arm about her shoulders and turned her back to the valley below. The sunlight was as bright as crystal, the sky as blue as baby bunting, the snow the purest white imaginable. Even the brown and gray of the stony ground and the green of the trees seemed deep and vibrant colors, clean somehow and brimming with life. "We'll have a real family Christmas next year," Morgan said with something like wonder.

She lifted her arm about his waist. "Yes."

"And every year after that." He looked down at her. "Before long our lives will be overflowing with family, even grandchildren one day, though you'll be the youngest granny imaginable."

Her chin trembled. "I never thought to be anyone's granny after Jeremy died."

"I never thought I'd be the man my own father was, but now I think...I think I just might be one day."

"He would be so proud of you," she told him.

He wiped at his eyes and chuckled. "I'm rather proud of myself at the moment."

"I keep seeing them, you know, how you described them that day, Ben and Jeremy, hand in hand, and ever since then, I've seen us the same way."

He pulled her close and tucked her head beneath his chin. They held each other, gazing out over that valley, their breath frosting in the Christmas air, knowing that they would go inside soon and drink the last of Ben's cider in the healing warmth that had less to do with the fire laid on the hearth than the love that survived all. It was so much, so very much. It was, in fact, everything.

*   *   *   *   *

Arlene James has another heartwarming story for you next month. Look for
MARRYING AN OLDER MAN.
Coming in March
from Silhouette Special Edition.

Silhouette ROMANCE™

A PROTECTOR, A PROVIDER, A FRIEND AND A LOVER—HE'S EVERY WOMAN'S HERO....

He's My Hero

February 1999 MR. RIGHT NEXT DOOR
by Arlene James (SR #1352)

Morgan Holt was everything Denise Jenkins thought a hero should be—smart, sexy, intelligent—and he had swooped to her rescue by pretending to be her beloved. But if Morgan was busy saving Denise, who was going to save Morgan's heart from *her* once their romance turned real?

March 1999 SOLDIER AND THE SOCIETY GIRL
by Vivian Leiber (SR #1358)

Refined protocol specialist Chessy Banks Bailey had thirty days to transform rough 'n rugged, true-grit soldier Derek McKenna into a polished spokesman. Her mission seemed quite impossible...until lessons in etiquette suddenly turned into lessons in love....

April 1999 A COWBOY COMES A COURTING
by Christine Scott (SR #1364)

The last thing Skye Whitman intended to do was fall for a cowboy! But tempting rodeo star Tyler Bradshaw was hard to resist. Of course, her heart was telling her that it was already too late....

Enjoy these men and all of our heroes every month from

Silhouette®

Available at your favorite retail outlet.

Look us up on-line at: http://www.romance.net

SRHMH

If you enjoyed what you just read,
then we've got an offer you can't resist!

Take 2 bestselling love stories FREE!

Plus get a FREE surprise gift!

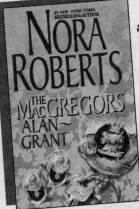
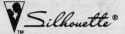

Silhouette
ROMANCE™

COMING NEXT MONTH

#1354 HUSBAND FROM 9 TO 5—Susan Meier
Loving the Boss
For days, Molly Doyle had thought she was Mrs. Jack Cavanaugh, and Jack played along—then she got her memory back, and realized she was only his *secretary*. So how could she convince her bachelor boss to make their pretend marriage real?

#1355 CALLAGHAN'S BRIDE—Diana Palmer
Virgin Brides Anniversary/Long Tall Texans
Callaghan Hart exasperated temporary ranch cook Tess Brady by refusing to admit that the attraction they shared was more than just passion. Could Tess make Callaghan see she was his truelove bride before her time on the Hart Ranch ran out?

#1356 A RING FOR CINDERELLA—Judy Christenberry
The Lucky Charm Sisters
The last thing Susan Greenwood expected when she went into her family's diner was a marriage proposal! But cowboy Zack Lowery was in desperate need of a fiancée to fulfill his grandfather's dying wish. Still, she was astonished at the power of pretense when *acting* in love started to feel a lot like *being* in love!

#1357 TEXAS BRIDE—Kate Thomas
Charming lawyer Josh Walker had always wanted a child. So when the woman who saved him from a car wreck went into labor, he was eager to care for her and her son. Yet lazy days—and nights—together soon had Josh wanting to make Dani *his*...forever!

#1358 SOLDIER AND THE SOCIETY GIRL—Vivian Leiber
He's My Hero
Refined protocol specialist Chessy Banks Bailey had thirty days to transform rough 'n' rugged, true-grit soldier Derek McKenna into a polished spokesman. Her mission seemed quite impossible...until lessons in etiquette suddenly turned into lessons in love....

#1359 SHERIFF TAKES A BRIDE—Gayle Kaye
Family Matters
Hallie Cates didn't pay much attention to the new sheriff in town—until Cam Osborne arrested her grandmother for moonshining! Hallie swore to prove her grandmother's innocence. But she was soon caught up in the strong, passionate arms of the law herself!